Joe DiMaggio

Young Sports Hero

Illustrated by Robert Brown

Joe DiMaggio

Young Sports Hero

by Herb Dunn

ALADDIN PAPERBACKS

First Aladdin Paperbacks edition September 1999

Aladdin Paperbacks
An imprint of Simon & Schuster Children's Publishing Division
1230 Avenue of the Americas
New York, NY 10020

Library of Congress Catalog Card Number: 99-65047

ISBN 0-689-83186-2

Illustrations

Contents

The Lost Boy

"Where's Giuseppe?"

"It's *Joe,* Papa!" twenty-year-old Mamie DiMaggio corrected her father, hollering from one side of their boat to the other. "In America, they say *Joe,* not Giuseppe."

"I named the boy *Giuseppe* like my father named *me* Giuseppe," Mr. DiMaggio hollered back in Italian. "I'll call him by the name I gave him. Anyway, where *is* he? I need him to pull up these nets and cut bait."

"Beats me," nineteen-year-old Thomas

DiMaggio answered, throwing a big fishing net over the side of the boat.

"I haven't seen him," added eighteen-year-old Marie DiMaggio as she repaired a hole in another net with a needle and thread.

"He's probably out playing ball," sixteen-year-old Michael DiMaggio yelled emptying a net full of salmon into a bucket. "He never wants to work."

"Maybe he went for a swim," joked twenty-six-year-old Nellie DiMaggio. She chuckled as she cleaned some bass with a sharp knife. Her fourteen-year old sister Frances giggled.

"That's not fair!" complained little Dominic DiMaggio. "How come I always have to work on the boat while Joe gets to have fun? I'm only seven!"

"Oh, hush, all of you," Rosalie DiMaggio told her children. "Joey is a good boy. He's just different."

The boat bobbed gently up and down in the waters of San Francisco Bay. Scattered across the bay were similar fishing boats, most of them owned by Italian immigrants like Giuseppe DiMaggio.

It was a cloudy Saturday in 1924. World War I had ended six years earlier. World War II would not explode in Europe for another fifteen years. Humankind had not landed on the moon yet. In fact, in 1924 nobody had even flown an airplane across the Atlantic Ocean.

At the rear of the DiMaggio fishing boat, all by himself, was ten-year-old Joe DiMaggio. His brothers and sisters may have thought he was having fun, but he wasn't.

Joe gripped the rail tightly and leaned over. Unlike the rest of the DiMaggio family, he didn't like the smell of fish. It nauseated him. Unlike the rest of the DiMaggio family, he didn't enjoy the feeling of being on a boat as it rose and fell and tilted with each ripple of water beneath its hull. He got seasick.

Joe's face was twisted into a scowl. He put his hand over his stomach and rubbed it, hoping that might make him feel better.

It didn't. He closed his eyes. Then he leaned farther over the rail and threw up.

Looking at this sick little boy, who ever would have believed that he would grow up to become one of the most famous Americans of the twentieth century?

The DiMaggios Come to America

It was getting dark outside as the sun sank in the west. The DiMaggio family had been up since four o'clock in the morning. They had caught, cleaned, and sold as many fish as they possibly could in one day.

Exhausted, they lined up and carefully wiped their dirty shoes on the mat outside their little house before setting foot inside. The DiMaggios lived at the bottom of a three-story building at 2047 Taylor

Street in the North Beach section of San Francisco. They didn't have a car, so they all walked home from Fisherman's Wharf.

As Mr. DiMaggio and his children washed their hands over and over again trying to clean off the fish, Mrs. DiMaggio prepared dinner.

"What are we having tonight, Ma?" asked little Dominic, the youngest of the children.

"Fish."

"Why do we always have fish?"

"Because we're fishermen," interrupted Mr. DiMaggio. "That's why we have fish."

"We don't *always* have fish," Mrs. DiMaggio reminded Dominic. "We usually have spaghetti."

"Fish and spaghetti. Fish and spaghetti," Dom complained. "Can't we have steak once in a while?"

"No," Mr. DiMaggio said firmly. He shot Dom a look but wasn't too hard on the boy, because he was so young.

14

"*Why* can't we have steak once in a while?"

"Because I said so."

"Steak is very expensive, Dominic," Mrs. DiMaggio explained, more gently than her husband. "Your father is not a millionaire, you should know."

"You're lucky we have any food at all," Mr. DiMaggio said. "There are lots of families that have *nothing* to eat tonight. You should be thankful."

Michael DiMaggio nudged his sister Marie. "Here we go again," he whispered.

"I heard that, Michael," Mr. DiMaggio said sternly. "You don't know how lucky you kids have it. When I was a boy in Italy, we would go days without food."

The older children rolled their eyes. They had heard the story so many times before that they knew it by heart. Joe and Dom, just ten and seven, were fascinated.

"No food at all?" Dom asked, amazed.

"Your mama and I were born in Sicily,"

Mr. DiMaggio explained. "It's an island in southern Italy."

"Your papa and I met as children," Rosalie DiMaggio continued, "in Isola Della Fammine, a small island northwest of Palermo in the Golfo di Carini—"

"For two hundred years, the DiMaggios were fishermen," Mr. DiMaggio interrupted, taking over. "But times were very hard, and it was tough to make a living over there. We wanted a better life. Everybody wanted a better life.

"So what did you do?" asked Dominic.

"We heard there was opportunity in America. The American dream we heard so much about. They said that in America, you can be anything you want to be if you work hard enough for it. I can work very hard."

"Enough ancient history, Pop," Vince said. "Get to the part where we were born."

"Not so fast," Mr. DiMaggio said, shooting one of his looks at Vince. "Your grandpa

16

made a trip to America to see for himself. He didn't find the streets were paved with gold as some people said, but he found there *was* honest work to be done here. There were jobs. And the fishing was good off the coast of San Francisco. In 1898 he sent for me."

"What about Mom?" Dom asked.

"Your mama was . . . in the family way."

"What does that mean, Pop?" Dom asked.

"She was pregnant," Nellie explained to the younger children. "She was going to have a baby."

Mrs. DiMaggio picked up the story. "We decided that Giuseppe would come to America for one year. At the end of that year, if he felt he could build a life here, I would join him. If he didn't like it here, he would go back to Italy."

"So I guess you liked it, eh, Pop?"

"Not right away. I got a job as a laborer working on a railroad. Putting down track. Hammering in spikes. All day. For this, I was paid ten cents an hour."

17

"Ten cents!" Dom exclaimed. "What can you buy with ten crummy cents?"

"It adds up," Mr. DiMaggio said. "I saved my money, every penny I could."

"And then you brought mama over?"

"Not yet," Giuseppe went on. "I wasn't happy. I wasn't a railroad man. I was a fisherman. I needed to fish. It was the one thing I was really good at. Fishing was in my blood."

"This is the part where you made the boat, right, Dad?"

"Quiet. I didn't have any money to buy a boat, so I decided to build one. Every day, after work, I went home and worked on a little skiff. It took several months before I finished it. When it was done, I named it Rosalie, after your mama."

Mrs. DiMaggio blushed, and Giuseppe gave her a big kiss. The DiMaggio girls sighed and giggled. The boys moaned and said they felt sick.

"I found a little apartment in Martinez,

California, a fishing village twenty-five miles from San Francisco, on the eastern shore of the Bay," Giuseppe continued. "Soon, I was able to quit my job and devote all my time to fishing. When I had enough money, I sent for your mama to join me in California. She arrived with our first baby, and we named her Nellie."

"I was the only one who was born in Italy," Nellie informed the others.

"We were lucky. We never had to hire any employees," Giuseppe boasted. "You kids were the employees. Mamie was born in 1903, and then came Thomas in 1905, Marie in 1906, Michael in 1908, Frances in 1910, Vincent in 1912, Giuseppe in 1914—"

"That's me!" Joe announced, and everyone laughed.

"Hey, what about me?" whined Dominic.

"And, finally," Mr. DiMaggio said, "in February of 1917, Dom was born."

"Yeah!" Dom shouted.

"And that's how our family got started in the United States. We are Americans now. We are poor, but we are proud. We work hard. We don't make a lot of money, but we make enough to live. We don't have steaks, but we have food on our table. You don't have the finest clothes, but you have shirts on your backs."

Joe and Dom looked at each other. As the two youngest in a family of five boys, they had the most ragged clothes that had been handed down from Thomas to Michael to Vince.

"So everybody dig in," Mrs. DiMaggio said.

"I hate fish," Joe announced.

There was silence around the table. The children looked into their laps, afraid to look at one another or at their father. They were afraid that Joe might get a spanking for what he had said. But Mr. DiMaggio didn't punish his son. He was struggling to get used to the idea that Joe was different from the other children.

A Secret Project

The sun had not yet come up over the San Francisco Bay on Monday morning. The nine DiMaggio children and their parents were asleep in their little four-room apartment.

Joe shared a room with his brothers Vincent and Dominic. The four girls shared another room. Thomas and Michael shared a room. So did Mr. and Mrs. DiMaggio. Somehow, they all fit.

It was almost four o'clock in the morning when Giuseppe DiMaggio woke up without the help of an alarm clock. He pulled on his boots and scraped a straight razor against his face. When the time reached four-thirty, he was fully dressed and had finished eating his breakfast. He marched into the children's rooms.

"Time to get up!" Mr. DiMaggio announced. "Nellie! Mamie! Marie! Frances! Get up! Thomas! Michael! Get up! Vincent! Dominic! Giuseppe! Get up!"

Slowly the children rubbed the sleep from their eyes and shuffled into the kitchen for breakfast. All except Joe.

"Let's go, let's go!" Papa DiMaggio shouted, clapping his hands together. "It is a beautiful day to be out on the boat. The fish are waiting to be caught."

Joe opened one eye and quickly closed it. He saw nobody was looking at him. He pulled the covers over his head.

"Joe," Vincent whispered into his brother's ear. "Are you asleep?"

"Yeah," Joe mumbled.

"You'd better get up, Joe," Dominic said.

"I don't want to."

"Papa will be mad."

"I don't want to go," Joe moaned.

While the other DiMaggio children ate their breakfast, Joe pretended to be asleep.

"Where's Giuseppe?" asked Mr. DiMaggio. Vincent and Dominic glanced at each other.

"He must be asleep," Marie guessed.

"All he wants to do is sleep," Mr. DiMaggio complained. "He never wants to work."

"Let the boy sleep," Mrs. DiMaggio told her husband gently. "He's tired."

"Why is he so tired if he never works? DiMaggios are not lazy bums. We've been fishing for two hundred years and—"

"Everybody doesn't have to be a fisherman!" snapped Mrs. DiMaggio. She knew how to make her husband calm down.

"How come Joe gets to sleep before school and I have to get up to work?" Dom whined.

"Quiet, Dominic," Mrs. DiMaggio said, handing her youngest son a plate of eggs. "Eat your breakfast."

Mrs. DiMaggio tiptoed into Joe's room and knelt next to his bed. Joe kept his eyes closed. His mother ran her hand through his black hair and planted a soft kiss on his cheek. "You rest this morning, Joey. I know you don't like the fish. Don't worry. Stay home until it's time to go to school. I'll tell Papa you weren't feeling well."

Joe opened his eyes and smiled at his mother.

When the rest of the DiMaggio family had finished their breakfast and left the house, Joe jumped out of bed and put his ragged clothes on. He quickly ate some breakfast. He didn't want to waste a minute, because there was something very important he wanted to do that morning.

Last week, while he was poking around

near Fisherman's Wharf, he had found an old wooden oar in a trash can. The long, flat part had a big split down the middle, but the rest of the wood was solid. One of the fishermen probably had thrown the oar away. Joe had picked it up and brought it home. He'd hid it in the basement until he had some time to himself. Finally he had the time.

Down in the basement, Mr. DiMaggio kept some hand tools that he used to repair the fishing boat. Joe put the long oar into a vise and used a ruler to measure thirty inches from the round handle. He made a line with a pencil at that point and got out a handsaw. Carefully, he cut the oar. The flat end with the split in it fell to the floor.

Perfect, Joe thought as he opened the vise. He gripped the knob at the end of the oar with both hands and admired the piece of wood, then put it back into the vise.

Next, Joe took a wood plane and slid it along the thicker end of the wood. He shaved

one side down, then turned the piece of wood and shaved the other side. Curly slivers of wood flew off as he pushed the plane along the wood.

Every few minutes, Joe would stop to rest his arms and wipe his forehead with his T-shirt. It was hard work, but it didn't seem to bother him.

Joe loved his family, but he enjoyed being by himself for a change. In fact, he didn't mind being alone at all. In a family of nine children, there was very little time for any of them to be by themselves.

Slowly, the thicker end of the wood became rounded. Joe shaved some of the wood off the handle to make that part thinner. He worked hard to make it perfectly round and smooth. Soon, it didn't look anything like the oar to a boat. It looked like what he wanted it to be: a baseball bat.

Joe had never owned a real baseball bat. They cost a lot of money, and Joe didn't have any money. Even if he did, he knew his father would never approve of spending money on such a silly, useless thing. As soon as Joe had seen the broken oar in the trash can, he had gotten the idea in his head to carve it into a baseball bat.

When Joe had made the bat as round as he could with the wood plane, he took the bat out of the vise. He looked around until he found a piece of sandpaper. He wrapped it around the bat and slid it up and down the barrel. Little by little, the bumps and pits in the wood disappeared. The bat was so smooth that Joe could run his finger along it without getting a splinter.

Perfect, he thought again.

Joe gripped his homemade bat with both hands and held it up. He took an imaginary batting stance at an imaginary home plate and stared down an imaginary pitcher. Joe had never seen a real baseball game, but he'd heard many of them on the radio. He had seen pictures of Babe Ruth, the famous slugger who played for the New York Yankees.

Just three years ago, in 1921, the "Bambino" had hit an amazing fifty-nine home runs. That was more than anyone had ever hit in a single season. People said that someday Babe might even hit sixty.

"Maybe someday I'll hit home runs for the Yankees," Joe said to himself as he pumped his bat back and forth. He couldn't wait to show the bat to Vincent and Dominic.

Wait a minute! Vince and Dom were probably at school by now! Joe had lost track of the time. He carefully hid his bat behind a box and rushed upstairs. He grabbed his books and ran off to school.

Crazy Game

Most of the students at Hancock Grammar School were children of poor Italian immigrants, like the DiMaggios. Joe always sat in the back row of his fifth-grade class. His teacher, Mrs. Lombard, was a nice lady.

But Joe didn't like school. He didn't raise his hand unless he was really sure he knew the answer to a question. He didn't like to be called on in class. He felt uncomfortable talking in front of everyone. He was afraid he might say something foolish and the other children would laugh at him.

"Who can name all the continents?" Mrs. Lombard asked as she paced back and forth in front of her students. Some of the students raised their hands. Mrs. Lombard picked a small girl with dark hair to give the answer.

"North America, South America, Europe, Asia, Africa, Antarctica, and Australia," the girl chirped proudly.

"Good," said Mrs. Lombard. "Now tell me, who can name all the oceans?"

A boy raised his hand, and Mrs. Lombard called on him.

"The Atlantic, Pacific, Arctic, Indian, and Antarctic," he said, very proud of himself.

"Correct," said Mrs. Lombard. "Now let's see. Here's a tough one. Who can name all the cities that have a team in the American League?"

A bunch of hands shot up in the air. Joe DiMaggio's was not one of them. Joe had not been paying attention. He was doodling pictures in his notebook. He drew pictures of baseball fields and baseball players. Pictures of the new bat he had made. He hadn't even noticed when Mrs. Lombard walked around to the back of the class and peeked at what he was doing.

"Joe," Mrs. Lombard asked. "Do you know the answer to the question I just asked?"

Joe heard his name called and looked up suddenly. Everyone was staring at him.

"Uh, no," he said. "I don't know the answer."

Some of the kids giggled. Joe felt his face turning red. This was just the situation that he hated. This was why he didn't like school. He wished he could disappear.

"Joe, you really don't know the names of the eight teams in the American League?"

"Oh, I know *that*," Joe replied. Then he quickly rattled them off: "Washington Senators, New York Yankees, Detroit Tigers, St. Louis Browns, Philadelphia Athletics, Cleveland Indians, Boston Red Sox, and Chicago White Sox."

"Very good."

Joe breathed a sigh of relief. At least he hadn't made a total fool of himself.

At the end of class, Mrs. Lombard asked Joe to stay behind after the other kids left the room. "I saw what you were drawing in your notebook," she said.

"I'm sorry, Mrs. Lombard."

"Joe, what do you want to be when you grow up?"

"A professional baseball player," he replied right away.

Mrs. Lombard laughed, then she realized Joe was completely serious. "If you want to succeed as a professional ballplayer," she explained, "you've got to give it your full attention, Joe. Baseball is a mental game. You've got to be thinking all the time. Right? What's the count? How many outs are there? What should I do if the ball is hit to me? Should I run or hold my base? You've got to be thinking all the time. Do you see what I mean?"

34

Joe didn't realize that his teacher knew so much about baseball. "Yes, Mrs. Lombard," he replied.

"School is the same way, Joe," Mrs. Lombard continued quietly. "You've got to be thinking all the time. And not just about baseball."

"Yes, Mrs. Lombard."

After school, Joe rushed back down to the basement. His new bat was right where he'd left it. Joe took a roll of old white tape and wound it around the handle in a spiral about ten inches up from the knob. This would help him get a better grip on the bat. It would prevent the wood from splitting, too.

When he heard his brothers and sisters had come home from school, he couldn't resist showing them what he had made. All the DiMaggio children loved to play sports, and they all gathered around him to see what he had.

"That's a nice bat, Joe," Michael complimented him. "It looks like it was made by a pro."

"Will you pitch to me?"

"I would, but I don't have a ball," Michael said.

"Joe made the bat," Thomas said. "He can make a ball, too."

Thomas, who was nineteen, was the best athlete in the family. He had played on a few amateur teams. He found a small, round stone in front of the house and picked up the roll of tape Joe had used to wrap the bat. He rolled the tape around and around the stone until it was about the same size as a baseball. Then he took a rag and wrapped it tightly around the tape, putting a few stitches of thread into it to hold it together.

"There you go," Thomas said when he had finished. "Just like a major-league ball."

They went out to the narrow alley behind their house. Thomas picked up a rock and scraped it along the wall to make a rectangle the size of a strike zone.

"If I throw the ball in this box, it's a strike," Thomas said. "If it's not in the box, it's a ball. Got it?"

"What if I hit it?" Joe asked.

"Don't worry," Thomas explained as he paced off sixty feet. "A pipsqueak like you ain't gonna hit my pitching."

"Maybe you should get your glove," Joe suggested.

"What for?"

Joe went over to the rectangle Thomas had drawn on the wall and took his batting stance. He took a few practice swings. The bat felt good in his hands.

"You ready, Bambino?" Thomas asked. Joe nodded his head and got ready.

Thomas went into his windup and let the pitch fly. It skipped off the concrete, too low to be a strike. Joe started to swing, but held up just in time.

"Good eye," Thomas said as the ball rolled back to him. "Never swing at a pitch unless it's in the strike zone. If pitchers see that you'll swing at bad pitches, they'll never throw you a good one."

Thomas went into his windup once again. This time, he threw the ball into the strike zone. And this time, Joe took a swing.

The ball rocketed off Joe's bat right up the middle, directly at Thomas's head. Thomas put one hand up to protect his face but realized almost instantly that without a glove he could break one of his fingers. He ducked and fell backwards, the ball missing his skull by a few inches.

"Maybe I'd better get my glove," Thomas said.

Thomas pitched to Joe for about half an hour, then said he had to go help their father on the boat. By that time, Michael had come home. He was also a good ballplayer, and he pitched to Joe for a while. Michael threw hard, but Joe was able to get a piece of the ball on just about every pitch. He pretended he was a right-handed Babe Ruth, slamming pitch after pitch into the bleachers at Yankee Stadium.

When Michael got tired, Vince and Dom took over. When Vince and Dom had had enough, Joe begged his sister Frances to pitch and play catch with him. By this time, the homemade baseball was dirty brown, lumpy, and starting to fall apart.

"Joe," Frances complained after a while, "my arm is falling off!"

"Just one more?" Joe begged.

When Frances refused to throw another pitch, Joe carefully cleaned the marks off his bat with a rag and brought it into his room. He put it under his bed so it would be safe.

Soon it was dinnertime. Mr. and Mrs. DiMaggio came back from the boat. While Mrs. DiMaggio prepared dinner, the children started working on their homework. Joe was sitting at the kitchen table with Dom and

Vincent when their father came up from the basement. He was holding the split end of the oar Joe had cut off to make his baseball bat. He had an angry look on his face. "What's this?" he asked.

The boys looked at each other, then peeked at Joe to see what he would do. "It's a broken oar, Papa," Joe said. "I found it in the garbage over by Fisherman's Wharf."

"I could have fixed this oar and used it on the boat, Giuseppe," Mr. DiMaggio said, with some annoyance in his voice. "Why did you cut it up?"

"I made something out of it," Joe explained. He went to his room and took the bat out from under his bed. He was proud of it. He thought that when his father saw the nice woodworking job he had done, he would be proud of Joe, too. He showed the bat to his father.

"What's that?" Mr. DiMaggio asked.

"A baseball bat, Papa," Joe said. "I carved

it myself. Just like you built your first boat when you came to America."

"I built my boat so I could fish," Mr. DiMaggio replied. "What do you need a baseball bat for?"

"To *hit*, Papa!"

Joe could tell right away that his father didn't approve of what he had done. Mr. DiMaggio scrunched up his face into a frown. "Crazy game," he said. "You hit a ball with a piece of wood and run around like a lunatic. Where's the sense in that? If you have to play a game, why don't you play soccer? When I was growing up in Italy, I played soccer with my friends."

"I like baseball better, Papa."

"This isn't Italy," Mrs. DiMaggio interrupted. "Let the boy play what he wants to play."

Mr. DiMaggio shook his head and took the piece of wood back down the basement. "I'm going to get the nets ready for tomorrow. There are fish waiting to be caught."

Catch Fish, Not Baseballs

A few blocks from the DiMaggio house on Taylor Street was a big field. It wasn't a nice, smooth, grassy field. It was filled with rocks and crabgrass, and bare patches of dirt. Back in 1906, a tremendous earthquake had wiped out much of San Francisco. The building that used to be at this spot was destroyed.

All the kids in the neighborhood called the field "the horse lot" because a local dairy parked its milk wagons there at night. To the poor immigrant children of the North Beach section of San Francisco, the horse lot was the place to hang out after school and in the summer. There was almost always a baseball game going on there.

The older DiMaggio kids didn't spend too much time at the horse lot. They were busy working on the boat with their parents or playing with friends their own age.

But Vince and Dom, like Joe, didn't enjoy fishing very much. They were still young, and weren't expected to devote themselves to the family business full time. All three boys loved baseball, and spent most of their spare time at the horse lot. If there was a game going on, they tried to get into it. If there was no position for another player, they would play catch with each other until one of the players went home.

One Saturday, Joe, Vince, and Dom went to the horse lot to see what was going on. When they got there, the field was being used by a bunch of older guys, men in their twenties. The DiMaggio brothers watched them practicing from the side.

"Those guys are good," Vince said after one of the players made a nice catch.

"Look how big that guy is," marveled Dom.

The game was about to start. The captains of the two teams met at home plate. The DiMaggio boys couldn't hear what they were saying, but Joe figured it out. "That team only has eight players," he told his brothers. "They need one more guy."

The captain of the team looked around the horse lot and spotted the DiMaggio brothers. He walked over to them. "One of you runts wanna play right field?" he asked.

Joe, Dom, and Vince looked at each other.

"I got a bum leg," Vince said nervously. Joe knew that Vince's leg was fine. He was just afraid to play with much older players.

"I . . . don't think so," Dom said.

"I don't have a glove," Joe replied.

"We have an extra glove."

"Okay, I'll play," Joe said. As he ran out to take his position in right field, some of the players laughed.

"Hey, right fielder!" one of them shouted. "Ain't this your nap time?" Everyone laughed.

As Joe took his position in right field, his heart was pounding. He had played plenty of pickup games with his brothers, but most of these players were twice his age and twice his size. They threw the ball hard. And it was a real hardball, not some homemade ball held together with tape and an old rag.

Nobody hit the ball to Joe in the first inning. When he hustled off the field after the third out to take his place on the bench, his teammates kidded him about how small and skinny he was. Joe just laughed. He didn't get a chance to bat in the first inning, either, because he was last in the batting order.

In the second inning, somebody lined a single past the first baseman. Joe ran over and scooped the ball up. The hitter rounded first base.

"Go for second!" somebody shouted from the bench. "That punk can't throw!"

Joe took a hop forward and whipped the ball toward second base. The shortstop was waiting there, his glove outstretched. He didn't have to move the glove an inch. The ball arrived long before the runner, who was so astonished that he didn't even have the chance to slide. He was out by ten feet.

"Whoa!" somebody on Joe's team shouted. "Did you see that? The kid's got a gun!"

On the sidelines, Vince and Dom were whooping it up like it was the World Series.

"Nice throw, Joe!" Vince shouted.

"That kid is my brother!" boasted Dom.

The first time Joe got a chance to hit, he struck out. The ball came at him so much faster than he'd ever seen before, he just couldn't get his bat around quickly enough. The next time up, he swung faster but only managed a weak foul pop to the first baseman.

The game moved along, and nobody hit the ball to Joe. The other team was almost all right-handed batters, and righties usually hit the ball to left field. The one left-handed batter struck out each time up. Joe wanted to make a play badly.

In the ninth inning, Joe's team had a one-run lead. The other team got a runner to second base. There were two outs, and the left-handed batter came up. Joe got ready, in case the guy got his bat on the ball this time.

"This guy can't hit!"

"Strike him out!" somebody yelled, "and the game will be over."

"Watch out, right field!" the center fielder shouted to Joe. Joe moved back a few steps. If the batter hit the ball over his head, Joe thought, he would try to make the play off

the fence. If the batter hit a single his way, he would throw the ball home and try to get the runner out at the plate.

But the batter didn't hit a single. He hit a long, high drive to right field. With the crack of the bat, Joe knew the ball was over his head. He could tell that it was heading to his left. He started sprinting in that direction and back.

At the edge of the horse lot was a low, chain-link fence. Joe had climbed it plenty of times. He couldn't look at it, because he would lose sight of the ball. He had to guess where it was. As he ran back, Joe reached out with his bare hand to feel for the fence.

Five feet from the fence, Joe could see the ball coming down. He had a chance for it. He jumped and reached up as high as he could with his glove hand. The ball hit the glove, and Joe closed it tightly. His legs hit the top of the fence as he came down. The fence flipped him over, and he landed on the other side, on the sidewalk that surrounded the horse lot. He was dazed, but he wasn't hurt.

Lying on his back, he held his glove up in the air. The ball was in the webbing. The game was over.

Everyone on his team came running over to congratulate Joe on his great catch and to see if he was okay. Vince and Dom were hugging him and clapping him on the back.

"I ripped my pants," Joe said as he got to his feet shakily. "They must have torn on the fence when I landed."

"You caught the ball, and that's what counts," Vince told him.

"You won the game, Joe!" Dom said proudly.

When they got home, Mr. DiMaggio was washing up after a hard day of work. Mrs. DiMaggio, as always, it seemed, was hard at work in the kitchen. Various brothers and sisters were doing chores and helping their mother.

"You should have seen it, Mom!" Dom bubbled as he ran in with Joe and Vince. "Joe played in a game with a bunch of old guys! And he was great! He threw a guy out who was trying to stretch a single into a double and—"

Mr. DiMaggio came into the kitchen at that moment. Joe tried to cover his pants with his hand, but the first thing his father noticed was the long rip running down Joe's pant leg. "What happened?" he asked gruffly. "I pay good money to buy clothes for you kids. Then you go and ruin them."

"But, Pop, you should have seen it!" Dom continued. "Joe won the game! He was the hero! There was this long fly ball, and Joe jumped over the fence to catch the ball! The pants got ripped, but oh boy it was a beautiful play. Everybody was jumping up and down after he caught the ball!"

Mr. DiMaggio looked at Joe, unimpressed. "Catch fish," he said simply, "not baseballs."

Tough Choice

Today, people who live in California can go
see a major-league baseball game just about
any night of the week. There are teams
in Los Angeles, San Francisco, San Diego,
Ananheim, Oakland, and Seattle, Washington. But before the 1950s, there was no
big-league team on the West Coast. In fact,
there was no big-league team west of St.
Louis, Missouri.

There was no television, cable, or satellite
TV, either. When Joe DiMaggio was a boy, the
only way to see big-league ball in California

was to go to a movie theater and hope they showed a short "newsreel" about baseball.

But that didn't mean the DiMaggio brothers didn't see good baseball. The West Coast had a whole league of top-quality minor-league teams. It was called the Pacific Coast League. Many major leaguers played in the PCL before or after their careers.

The Pacific Coast League played a 187-game season, with teams in Los Angeles, Hollywood, Oakland, San Diego, Portland, Sacramento, Seattle, and, of course, San Francisco.

In fact, San Francisco had *two* teams, the Seals and the Missions. When young Joe DiMaggio went to bed at night, he didn't dream of playing in the majors. All he thought about was that someday he might be good enough to play for the Seals or the Missions.

In 1925, Joe was just eleven years old. All he could do was dream. But his oldest brother Thomas was twenty years old.

Working on his father's fishing boat had made him big and strong.

Like all the DiMaggio children, Thomas was also a good athlete. He didn't love baseball the way Joe, Dom, and Vince did. But he did play the game, and his little brothers were in awe of how far he could throw and hit a ball.

One night, at dinner, Thomas was very quiet. Joe was usually the quiet one in the family, but on this night Thomas didn't say a word. Something was bothering him.

"What's the matter?" Mrs. DiMaggio asked, putting a hand against Thomas's forehead. "Are you feeling okay?"

"I met a guy today," Thomas finally said. "The manager of the Seals."

Joe dropped his fork. Dom and Vince stopped eating and looked at Thomas expectantly.

"Seals?" asked Mr. DiMaggio. "What are Seals?"

"They're a baseball team," Dom explained excitedly.

Mr. DiMaggio snorted.

"He told me he's been watching me," Thomas said. "The Seals are interested in me."

"What did you tell him?" Dom asked. "Are they gonna sign you? What position will you play?"

Everyone at the table looked at Thomas.

"No," he said softly. "I told the guy I work with my dad. He needs me more than the Seals do. There would be no way Dad could run the business without my help."

"Good boy," Mr. DiMaggio said, his mouth full of food.

Joe, Vince, and Dom sank into their seats. They looked over at Thomas and saw the sad, sad look on his face.

The Jolly Knights

"C'mon Joe! Rip another one!"

"You can do it, Joe!"

"Over the wall and we win it all, Joe."

Joe DiMaggio stepped up to the plate. He set his feet very wide apart, much wider than anyone else on the Jolly Knights. While the pitcher fidgeted on the mound, Joe took a few smooth practice swings. He didn't lunge as he swung. He didn't flail awkwardly like a lot of the other boys.

Joe was thirteen years old now. From spending countless hours throwing, catching, and hitting with his brothers and sisters, he had developed his skills as a baseball player.

Joe stood like a statue waiting for the first pitch. He didn't twitch. He didn't wave the bat around menacingly. Unlike most of the other boys, Joe barely lifted his front foot off the ground as he swung. Without anyone coaching him, he had figured out that any extra movements only make it harder to get the bat on the ball and hit it solidly.

The pitcher went into his windup and delivered the ball. Joe watched it sail high, and the umpire called ball one.

Joe always waited until the last possible instant to swing the bat. Then he would extend his arms and slice his bat through the strike zone faster than any of the other boys. He had a big follow-through, but he didn't swing wildly and spin around the way some of the other kids did. Already, people watching him were saying that he had a beautiful swing.

The pitcher delivered again. This time, the ball was too low, but the umpire called it a strike. Joe knew it was a bad call, but he didn't argue. He knew that arguing with umpires never got you anywhere. In fact, it could hurt you. The next time up, the umpire might remember and pay you back for making him look bad.

The count was one ball and one strike. The boys on both teams were shouting encouragement to their teammates.

Joe was playing in his first organized league run by the local Boys Club. There was no Little League baseball when Joe DiMaggio was a boy. He had joined the Jolly Knights mainly because it was the only way he could use real equipment. For the first time in his life, he had a real leather baseball glove. Just like the guys on the San Francisco Seals.

The Jolly Knights had won almost all their games, but so had another team, the Vikings.

Now the two teams were playing for the Boys Club championship of San Francisco. Joe had hit a home run earlier in the game to put the Jolly Knights in the lead. But the Vikings caught up and tied the score. It was the last inning. The bases were empty.

The pitcher looked in for the sign and went into his windup. His pitch was a little outside, and Joe let it go by. This time the umpire made the right call. The count was two balls and one strike.

"You've got him now, Joe!"

"This is your pitch, Joe!"

The pitcher delivered once again, and this time Joe swung with all his might. But he missed.

"Strike two!" barked the umpire.

Joe choked up on his bat a little. With two strikes, he knew he had to protect the plate, just get the bat on the ball and hope he could knock it through the infield somewhere. The most important thing was not to strike out.

Joe didn't worry about striking out, though. He hardly ever missed three pitches in a row. Part of it was his skill. He was a good hitter. The other part of it was his confidence. He *knew* he was a good hitter. He was still very young, but already he felt he could hit any pitcher, catch any ball hit in his direction.

The pitch came in once again, and Joe could see right away it was straight over the middle of the plate, about belt high. He swung hard, and this time he felt his bat meet the ball. He hit it just below the center, which made it rise on a line.

Joe took off. He knew he hit it well, but at the moment of impact, it is impossible to tell if a ball is going to be caught, drop in for a hit, or go over the fence for a home run. Maybe the wind would hold it up, or maybe it would push it farther. When in doubt, Joe knew, *run*.

The ball was still in the air when Joe got to first. He had lost sight of it, but he saw the center fielder looking up and running back. Joe turned on the speed and headed for second.

Then, the center fielder stopped. He had no chance. The ball sailed over the fence.

The Jolly Knights had won the San Francisco Boys Club championship. Joe's teammates were off the bench and ready to mob Joe when he crossed the plate. Joyously they picked him up and carried him around the bases. Joe was too happy to be embarrassed being the center of attention.

At the end of the game, the president of the local Boys Club went out to the pitcher's mound to announce the Most Valuable Player of the game. The players of both teams lined up on the foul lines for the award ceremony.

"You won it, Joe," his teammate Frank Venezia whispered. "They have to give it to you."

"I don't want it," Joe whispered back.

"You're crazy," replied Frank. "Why not?"

"I don't want all those people looking at me."

"Boys!" boomed the Boy's Club president. "You played a great game. I wish I could give this Most Valuable Player award to all of you. I can't do that, so I had to select one. This year's Boys Club MVP is . . . Mr. Joe DiMaggio!"

"Frank," Joe whispered. "You go up there and accept it in my place."

Frank gave Joe a shove toward the pitcher's mound. The crowd around the field erupted into cheers. Joe was handed a gift certificate for sixteen dollars—a lot of money in 1927—and two gold-plated baseballs.

Embarrassed, Joe accepted the gifts and held them up over his head. He looked around the crowd and saw his sisters Nellie, Mamie, Marie, and Frances. His brothers Thomas, Michael, Vincent, and Dominic were there. Even his mother had come out to see the end of the game. But Joe's father was nowhere in sight.

Difficult Times

"Mr. DiMaggio!"

Joe DiMaggio looked up suddenly. His social studies teacher, Mr. Hawthorne, was glaring at him. "Have you been listening to a word I've been saying?"

Joe just hung his head. He knew that if he said yes, Mr. Hawthorne would ask him a question he couldn't answer. If he said no, he would be admitting he hadn't been paying attention, and all the other students would laugh. He couldn't win.

While his classmates at Francisco Junior

High School were listening to Mr. Hawthorne, Joe was catching imaginary fly balls and hitting imaginary home runs in his head. He tried to focus on reading and writing and social studies, but he kept thinking about double plays, foul tips, and stolen bases.

Joe was a star athlete on the school's baseball and tennis teams. But he was not a good student. He knew it, his teachers knew it, and his classmates knew it. Joe managed to get through junior high school, but he struggled the whole time and was a very unhappy student. He hoped that high school might be better, but in the back of his mind he didn't think it would be.

High school, as it turned out, was even worse for Joe. Classes were harder. There was more to read. Joe didn't think courses like biology and algebra and geometry were interesting. It seemed like there was a test every day.

But even worse than all that, Joe didn't feel like he fit in with his classmates. In grammar school and junior high, Joe attended schools right in his neighborhood. The kids in his classes were a lot like him—children of poor immigrants struggling to make a life for themselves in America.

But there was no high school in the North Beach section of San Francisco. The kids who lived there had to go to other parts of the city to attend school.

Galileo High School was in a section of San Francisco where a lot of wealthy families lived. From the first day of school there, Joe knew the students were different. It was the way they looked at him. Like they were better than he was.

For the first time, Joe became self-conscious about the unfashionable, hand-me-down clothes he was wearing. Some of the kids at Galileo even wore suits and ties to school!

Joe had never thought about it, but to the

other students his name was instantly recognized as being Italian. In the 1920s, being Italian meant that you were poor. Everybody knew it.

For the first time, Joe felt like the other kids at school were smarter than he was. They talked differently. They used words he didn't understand. Sometimes they would laugh when he spoke incorrectly. So he became even more quiet and shy than he was already.

Even though he continued to shine as an athlete for the Galileo baseball team, Joe hated high school and began thinking about the day he would be able to quit.

It was while Joe was at Galileo that one of the most important days in American history took place. On October 24, 1929, a month before Joe's fifteenth birthday, the stock market collapsed, and the economic system of the United States was thrown into a deep depression.

Almost overnight, millions of dollars that people had worked so hard to save had vanished. Thousands of people lost their jobs. Many had no money at all. This was the beginning of what came to be called the Great Depression.

The DiMaggios, who were already quite poor, had to suffer even more. They could catch a lot of fish. But if people did not have money, they couldn't afford to buy the fish that Mr. DiMaggio was selling. And if people didn't buy the fish, the DiMaggios would not earn money for food, clothes, and everything else a family with nine children needed every day.

The DiMaggio family had always worked to make ends meet. With America caught in the Depression, it became even more important for everyone in the family to contribute.

Joe didn't want to work on his father's fishing boat, so he did other things to earn

money for his family. He got a job as a delivery boy. That lasted a week or two. He worked down at the docks loading and unloading ships. That didn't last much longer. He even had a job squeezing oranges to make orange juice. He hated all of these jobs.

Even little Dominic DiMaggio, who was only twelve, was put to work. For a while, Joe and Dom got jobs selling the *San Francisco Chronicle* newspaper on street corners. The newspaper sold for three cents a copy. For each copy sold, the newsboy got to keep a penny. When they had sold a hundred papers, they had earned a dollar.

One dollar doesn't sound like a lot of money, but during the Depression people were happy to earn any money at all.

Joe wasn't very good at selling newspapers. He was naturally quiet. He didn't like shouting out the headlines and trying to get people on the street to buy a newspaper. Dominic was actually better than Joe at this job.

But no matter how many newspapers they sold, at the end of the day, Joe and Dom would count out their profits and bring it home to their parents to help pay the bills. Every little bit helped.

At the end of his freshman year of high school, Joe did some serious thinking. He had reached the age where a young man begins to decide what he wants to do with the rest of his life.

Joe didn't enjoy school and he wasn't any good at it. Going on to college was out of the question. He didn't like any of the jobs he had tried, either.

He realized there was only one thing that he really liked and was good at: playing baseball.

A Big Decision

"Joe, are you in there?" Frank Venezia shouted through the window. "You up?"

It was early that summer, a few days after school let out. Joe was sleeping late. He wouldn't have to sell his newspapers until the afternoon.

"Joe, it's me, Frank!"

Joe opened his eyes. He and his friend Frank had had a silly argument a few months before and hadn't spoken to one another since then. Joe was suspicious. Why would Frank suddenly be coming around? "What do you want?" he asked.

"Y'know Rossi Olive Oil Company?" Frank asked. "They're sponsoring a baseball team for the neighborhood. I'm the captain. How about joining up?"

Joe got out of bed and went to the window. In the last year he had grown tall and wiry, with long arms and legs. He was up to 130 pounds now.

"I gotta work," Joe said, poking his head through the window.

"The games will be at night, Joe!" Frank said. "There will be real equipment, real uniforms. All the best guys in the neighborhood are joining up, Joe. But we're going to need you on the team to win. Aw, come on, Joe, it will be fun!"

"I don't know . . . "

"Joe, I'm sorry about that argument we had," Frank said, almost pleading. "It was stupid."

Joe thought it over for a minute. Frank had

been his good friend before their argument, one of the few friends he had.

"Well, okay," Joe said, sticking out his hand to shake Frank's. "As long as you let me play shortstop."

"It's a deal!"

Actually, Joe was not the best shortstop in the world. He could scoop up grounders well enough, but his throwing wasn't very accurate. Infielders have to be able to make quick, sidearm throws to beat runners to first base. But when Joe made that play, you never knew where the ball was going to wind up.

When a batter hit a ground ball to Joe at shortstop, the people sitting behind first base would start to scatter. They knew that the throw was likely to come sailing over the first baseman's head and directly at theirs!

Although Joe had his troubles at shortstop, he made up for them at the plate. He could hit a baseball like no schoolboy his age. Fastball pitchers, curveball specialists, right handers, left handers, it didn't matter—Joe hit everybody.

The Rossi team won one game after another on the strength of Joe's bat. In the league championship against a team sponsored by Maytag Washing Machines, Joe slugged two home runs.

Fifteen-year-old boys who can hit baseballs 350 feet tend to get noticed. Managers of other teams began pulling Joe aside after games to talk to him. A few of them offered him money to play for their team. Even though he was too young, representatives of the San Francisco Seals and the San Francisco Missions started stopping by to watch Joe play.

Rumors about this skinny San Francisco kid named Joe DiMaggio were even starting to reach major-league teams like the Red Sox, the Cardinals, and the Yankees. If the rumors were to be believed, the kid's brothers Vince and Dom were almost as good as he was.

That summer, Joe made a big decision: He wouldn't return to high school in the fall.

Back in the 1930s, many young people did not earn their high school diplomas. But even so, Joe knew that his father would be upset.

"You didn't want to fish like Michael and Thomas," Giuseppe DiMaggio complained when Joe broke the news to him. "And you don't want to go to school, either." Mr. DiMaggio threw his hands up in the air.

"But, Pop," Joe said, "if I didn't have to spend so much time in school, I could be out earning money for the family."

"What money are you going to earn?" Mr. DiMaggio complained. "There are plenty of college boys who can't find work. What are *you* going to do that they can't do?"

"I'll get a job," Joe claimed. "And in my spare time I'll play baseball."

"Baseball?" Mr. DiMaggio had grown tired of hearing about baseball. His son Thomas had played baseball before giving it up to work on the fishing boat. Vincent was playing on semipro teams. And even little Dominic, now fourteen, spent all his time playing the game. Mr. DiMaggio couldn't understand the attraction to this silly American game.

"Calm down, Giuseppe!" Mrs. DiMaggio said. "Let Joe get the baseball out of his system."

"He shames the DiMaggio name with all this baseball!" Giuseppe thundered. "Everyone will be laughing at you. They'll say the DiMaggio boys don't want to work."

"They will not laugh," Joe insisted. "They'll cheer for me."

"You're stubborn!"

"Just like you!"

I Play and They Pay

Mr. and Mrs. DiMaggio thought that after a couple of years their sons would get tired of baseball. But they didn't. Vince, Joe, and Dom kept on playing.

When they weren't working to help pay the bills, they would play stickball on the streets, pickup games at the playground, or on organized leagues for a few dollars a game. It didn't matter to the boys. They just loved to play. After a while, Mr. and Mrs. DiMaggio realized there was no point in trying to prevent the boys from playing.

Then one day in the spring of 1932, twenty-year-old Vincent came home with an announcement. He gathered the family together in the living room to break the news. "I signed a contract with the San Francisco Seals today," he informed his family. "I'm going to be a professional baseball player. They're going to pay me one hundred fifty dollars a month."

The idea of a professional baseball player earning $150 a month may sound funny to you. Today, professional athletes are paid millions of dollars. Some of them can make $150 just to sign their name on a bat or a ball.

But during the Depression, $150 for a month's work was a lot of money. That was more than Mr. DiMaggio made on his fishing boat. He couldn't believe it. "They pay you that kind of money to play a game?" he scoffed. "What's the catch?"

"There is no catch, Papa," Vince replied. "I play, and they pay."

"I'll believe it when I see it," Mr. DiMaggio snorted.

But the other DiMaggio boys believed it. Michael and Thomas were the first to congratulate Vince. They were happy and sad at the same time. Both of them had been great athletes. Thomas had even been offered a tryout with the Seals. But both of them had chosen to work with their father on the fishing boat.

Dom, now fifteen, and Joe, seventeen, went to shake Vincent's hand. They were proud of their big brother, and also a little envious. They wished they were in his shoes.

"You guys are next," Vince told them. "If I can do it, you can do it."

"I can't believe you're going to play for the Seals," Dom marveled. "That's my dream."

"You aim too low," Vince told his brothers. "It won't be long before both of you guys are

better than I am. I can tell. If you keep practicing, you're going to be good enough to play
in the major leagues. It's only a matter of
time."

While Joe and Dom waited for their time
to come, they did whatever they could to
help their father support the family. They
sold newspapers, delivered groceries, loaded
trucks, and worked as laborers on the San
Francisco docks. It was long hours and hard
work, but it made their muscles strong.
Whenever they had the chance, they played
baseball.

The same spring that Vince joined the
Seals, Joe caught on with an amateur team
sponsored by the Sunset Produce Company.
Most of the players had been Joe's teammates on the Rossi Olive Oil team the year
before.

If Joe was great with the Rossi team, he
was spectacular with Sunset Produce. In
eighteen games, his batting average was an

unheard-of .632. In other words, in every ten at bats, he had more than six hits.

He also was awarded a pair of baseball shoes for being the best player in the league. Joe's fielding improved, too. He made almost every play at shortstop.

People noticed that he ran differently than most players. It was effortless, loping. He ran like he wasn't really trying, the way he did everything.

Toward the end of the season, a middle-aged man came out of the stands and walked over to Joe after a game. He asked if he could have a few minutes of Joe's time. Joe walked off to the side of the field with the man.

"I've been watching you play the field," the man said. "How do you do that?"

"Do what?" Joe asked.

"How do you manage to get to the ball at the exact same instant that the ball gets to you?" he asked. "I mean, you never dive for a ball. You just seem to get to every ball hit in your direction. I can't figure it out."

Joe scratched his head. He'd never thought about it before. It just came naturally to him. "Well," he explained, "if I run too slowly, I won't get there in time to make the play. And if I run too fast, I get there too early and have to stand around waiting for the ball to get there."

The man just shook his head in wonder. He had seen a lot of ballplayers in his time, but he had never seen one like Joe DiMaggio.

"Hey, mister," Joe asked. "Who are you, anyway?"

"Joe, my name is Fred Hoffman. I manage the Missions."

Joe knew the name. Fred Hoffman had been a reserve catcher for the New York Yankees from 1919 to 1925. When his big-league career was over, he was hired by the San Francisco Missions of the Pacific Coast League.

"What do you want with me?"

"Joe, I know your brother Vince plays for the Seals," Hoffman said. "We've got a little rivalry going between the Seals and the Missions. I think you may be even better than Vince in a few years. I'd like you to come play for the Missions. We're prepared to offer you one hundred fifty dollars a month."

Joe was speechless. Ever since he had carved that first bat out of a broken oar, his dream had been to play for the Pacific Coast League. Now he was being given that chance.

There was just one problem for Joe: With his brother on the Seals, how could he play for their arch rivals? Joe had become a Seals fan, and wanted to play on the same team as Vince. But if he passed up this offer, who knew if he would ever get another one?

"What do you say, Joe?"

"I have to talk to my brother," he told Hoffman.

84

An Offer

Back in 1932, there was no night baseball. Games were played in the afternoon. Joe knew the Seals were playing at Seals Stadium that afternoon, so he went over to the ballpark to see if he could ask Vince what he thought of the offer to join the Missions.

It wasn't until he arrived that he realized he'd forgotten to bring something: money. Joe went through all his pockets, but he couldn't find the fifty cents he would need to get into the Seals game. He walked around the ballpark for a few minutes.

On the right-field fence, Joe recalled, there were a few knotholes in the wood. Sometimes kids who couldn't afford a ticket would stand there and watch the game through the fence. It wasn't a great view, but you were close to the right fielder. Vince played right field for the Seals, so Joe figured he might be able to shout to him through the fence.

There weren't any little kids hogging the knothole, so Joe peered through it. The Seals were at bat, he could tell. Vince was in the dugout. Joe was peering through the little hole when somebody tapped him on the shoulder.

"Excuse me, young man. Aren't you Vince DiMaggio's little brother?" a man asked.

"Yeah, my name is Joe."

"I'm Spike Hennessy," the man said, extending his hand. "I'm a scout for the Seals. Joe, you should never stand on the outside looking in, unless it's a jail."

"Did I do something wrong?" Joe asked.

"Not at all," Hennessy replied, laughing. "Why don't you come inside with me?"

Spike Hennessy led Joe into the ballpark. Instead of giving him a seat in the bleachers, as Joe had expected, he led him to the offices of the San Francisco Seals. Hennessy tapped on a door and opened it for Joe.

A short, bald man was sitting behind a large desk. There were pictures of ballplayers all over the walls, some of them major leaguers. Joe took it all in without saying a word. He felt awkward, uncomfortable.

"So this is the great Joe DiMaggio I've heard so much about," the guy behind the desk said, smiling.

Embarrassed, Joe lowered his head.

"Joe, my name is Charlie Graham," the man said. "I'm the owner of the Seals."

Joe shook Graham's hand and accepted his invitation to take a seat.

"They told me you were quiet," Graham said.

Joe didn't say a word in reply.

"Well, that's fine with me," Graham said, laughing. "I'm hoping your bat will do the talking for you."

"What do you mean?" Joe asked.

"We've been watching you and Vince and your little brother Dom for quite some time, Joe."

"You have?" Joe was astonished. It never had occurred to him that a big team like the San Francisco Seals would bother paying any attention to neighborhood kids.

"Oh, yes. Joe, do you know how the Seals make most of our money?"

"Uh, by selling tickets to the games?" Joe guessed.

"No."

"By selling hot dogs and peanuts?"

"Nope. Those are just sidelines. Joe, we stay in business by developing young players such as yourself and selling them to major-league teams when they're good enough. We

think you're a pretty good ballplayer just like your brother Vince. In fact, we think you're *very* good. Mr. Hennessy here tells me he thinks you'll be playing in the big leagues someday."

Joe couldn't believe what he was hearing. First the Missions offered him a job, and now the Seals were after him, too. It was too good to be true. "Are you saying you want me to play for the Seals, Mr. Graham?"

"Joe, that's exactly what I'm saying."

At that point, Spike Hennessey interrupted. "Joe," he said, "we know that the Missions are also interested in you."

"How do you know that?" Joe asked.

"We've got our eyes and ears open," Hennessey replied.

"We will match any offer the Missions have made," Graham said. "I have a contract right here."

"Where do I sign?" Joe asked, reaching for the pen.

Extra Bases

When Joe joined the San Francisco Seals at the end of the 1932 season, they were having a miserable year. The team had lost many more games than it had won, and was buried in last place of the Pacific Coast League.

The manager of the team was a man named Ike Caveney, who had once been the shortstop for the Cincinnati Reds. When he was introduced to seventeen-year-old Joe DiMaggio, he sat down and told the boy what to expect. Joe would sit on the bench,

Caveney explained. He just wanted Joe to watch and learn.

The Seals' shortstop, Augie Galan, was one of the best players in the league. In fact, he would go on to a sixteen-year career in the major leagues and hit one hundred home runs.

Joe didn't like riding the bench, but he understood how the game worked. Rookies had to wait their turn. Just because he was the star of the Sunset Produce team didn't mean he would be the star of the San Francisco Seals.

There were four games left in the season when Joe joined the Seals, and the players were thinking ahead to what they were going to be doing during the off-season. After the game, Augie Galan told manager Caveney he wanted to leave the team early. With the Seals deep in last place, Caveney gave Galan permission to go home.

Manager Caveney paced up and down the

Seals' locker room. He needed a shortstop to replace Augie Galan. He tried to figure out a way to juggle his lineup around to fill the position. No matter how he moved his players in his mind, he wasn't satisfied.

"Hey, Skip," said right fielder Vince DiMaggio. "My kid brother can play short."

The manager looked at Joe DiMaggio, sitting quietly at the corner of the locker room. Joe's uniform was completely clean because he hadn't been in a game yet. He looked so young that some people visiting the Seals' locker room figured he must be the batboy.

"DiMaggio!" Caveney barked at Joe. "You're playing short tomorrow."

Joe was so excited, he couldn't eat dinner that night. When he went to bed, he couldn't sleep. He just lay there, thinking about what he would do if a ball was hit to him. He practiced his batting stance in his mind.

As he put on his uniform the next day, he was so nervous, he was afraid he might not be able to play. His teammates greeted him, but Joe could barely croak out a response. When the Seals ran out on the field to take their positions, Joe prayed that nobody would hit the ball to short. Fortunately, nobody did. Joe relaxed a little.

In the second inning, there were two outs and the batter slapped a grounder toward the middle of the diamond. Instinctively Joe dashed to his left and reached for the ball. It landed in his glove. He set himself and made an accurate throw to first base to throw out the hitter by a step. His teammates pounded him on the back as they ran into the dugout.

When Joe stepped up to the plate for his first at bat as a professional baseball player, it was almost as if he were in a trance. It didn't seem real. He was just a poor San Francisco kid, and here he was hitting for the Seals. It seemed as if he were in a movie.

On the pitcher's mound was Herman Pillette, a veteran who when he was younger had won thirty-four games in three years for the Detroit Tigers. Pillette no longer had an overpowering fastball, but he was a very smart pitcher with good control.

Joe, nearly paralyzed with fear, let the first pitch go by. Pillette guessed the rookie would look at a pitch or two, so he put the ball right over the plate for strike one.

Joe watched the next pitch, too, and it was outside for ball one.

Pillette went into his windup, and Joe got ready for the next pitch. It looked good, and Joe, anxious, took a cut at it. He swung a little early, but he made contact.

The ball took off like a bullet down the left-field line. It was a fair ball by a few inches. The third baseman dove for it, but couldn't come up with it.

For an instant, Joe hesitated in the batter's box. He could hardly believe it. He had gotten a hit off a real, live, ex-major-league pitcher! He almost forgot to run.

Quickly, Joe tore out of the batter's box and sprinted for first. The first-base coach was waving him to second, but Joe didn't need to be told that. He knew the ball had made it past the infield. He rounded the base and chugged for second.

On the way to second, Joe caught a glimpse of the left fielder still chasing the ball down in the corner. A double was good, but a triple was better. Joe pushed off the second base bag without slowing down and headed for third.

It was going to be close, Joe knew. Ten feet from third base, he went into a slide, kicking up a cloud of dust. Safe! When Joe looked up for the umpire's call, the ball hadn't even arrived at the third baseman yet.

Joe thought he would be congratulated for hitting a triple in his first at bat, but the Seals' third-base coach was furious with him. "Open your eyes, rookie!" he yelled. "You didn't have to slide. I was signaling for you to come in standing up! Let's pay some attention out there!"

Joe felt bad that he hadn't paid attention to the third-base coach. But he felt good at the same time. He had actually gotten an extra-base hit off a major-league pitcher! He was good enough to play with these guys.

All the nervousness that Joe had felt was gone. When he went out to take the field in the next inning, he wasn't praying the ball would be hit elsewhere. He was praying it would be hit to him.

Take Me out to the Ball Game

"Pop, I want to show you something," Vincent DiMaggio said, carrying a brown suitcase into the kitchen.

The 1932 season had ended. Vince had played right field for the Seals all year, and Joe had played shortstop for the final three games. He hadn't been the best shortstop in the world, but he had handled most of the balls that had come his way. And he'd hit the ball hard.

"What is it, Vincent?" Mr. DiMaggio asked.

Vince clicked opened the suitcase. It was filled with dollar bills—1,500 of them. That may not sound like a fortune today, but Mr. DiMaggio had never seen so much money at one time in his life. The bills were stacked in neat piles.

"It's for you, Pop," Vince said. "I want you to have it."

"Who did you steal it from?" Mr. DiMaggio exploded. "I didn't raise my sons to be thieves! You're giving this money back right now!"

"I didn't steal it!" Vince laughed. "I *earned* it. Playing baseball. Pop, you've got to believe me. There's more money in baseball than there is in fishing."

Mr. DiMaggio picked up a stack of dollar bills and ran his thumb along the edges to make the bills flap. He let out a whistle. "They paid you all this money just to play a game?" he asked.

"Yeah, and more," Vince explained. "I had to spend some of it, too."

Mr. DiMaggio looked at Vince, who had grown taller and more muscular than his father. "I want you to take me to one of these baseball games," he said.

Joe and Dom just about fainted when Vince told them their father wanted to see a baseball game in person. All through their childhoods, Mr. DiMaggio had never shown the least interest in baseball. He had never been to a game. It was almost like he blamed baseball for the fact that his three youngest sons didn't want to follow in his footsteps and become fishermen.

The season was already over, so the boys couldn't take their father to see a Seals game. But there was always some kind of a game going on at Seals Stadium, so the DiMaggio brothers brought their father over one Sunday afternoon to see his first baseball game.

Two semipro teams were on the field, in the middle of a game. There were some people scattered in the stands, mostly friends or relatives of the players. Mr. DiMaggio and his sons took seats on the first base side.

"Look, it's a very simple game," Vince explained to his father. He and Dom and Joe pointed out the positions on the field and told their father that the player holding the bat was going to try to hit the ball where it couldn't be fielded.

"You see that pitch there?" Vince said. "It was too high for the batter to hit. That was a ball. Ball one."

"Of *course* it was a ball," Mr. DiMaggio snorted. "What else could it be? They play the game with a ball. I know *that* much."

The pitcher threw the next pitch over the plate. The umpire held out his arm and hollered, "Strike!"

"Yeah," Joe said. "But, Pop, if the pitcher

throws it over the plate like he just did, it's not a ball, it's a strike."

"Not a ball?" asked Mr. DiMaggio, puzzled.

"No," said Dom. "He still throws a *ball*, but they call it a strike."

"But you said it's not a ball," complained Mr. DiMaggio.

Vince, Joe, and Dom looked at each other. Explaining the game of baseball to their father was not going to be as easy as they had thought.

"Pop," Vince said, "what we said was that he *throws* a ball, but it's called a strike if it goes over the plate."

"How can it go from being a ball to not being a ball just because of where you throw it?" asked Mr. DiMaggio, who seemed to be getting a little frustrated.

"Trust us, Pop," Joe said. "It just does."

"It still looks like a ball to me," said Mr. DiMaggio. "But it was a strike?"

"Now you're catching on, Pop," Dom said.

Mr. DiMaggio shook his head and pulled out a handkerchief to wipe his forehead. "This game makes no sense at all."

"Sure it does, Pop," Joe said. "It's easy."

By that time, the batter had taken three more pitches out of the strike zone and jogged to first base. Dom tried to explain that the batter had walked. But Mr. DiMaggio had already lost interest. He looked around the stands at the fans watching the game. "So many people come to watch you play?" he asked.

"More than this," Vince replied. "At some of our games there are five thousand people."

"They pay to watch this?"

"Sure, Pop," Joe said. "They buy a lot of hot dogs and soda pop, too."

"Some of that money goes to the players?" Mr. DiMaggio asked, trying hard to understand.

"That's how I got the fifteen hundred bucks I showed you," Vince explained.

Mr. DiMaggio looked around the stands again. "Maybe this baseball thing isn't so bad after all," he said.

The First Streak

When the 1933 baseball season began, Joe was excited. This would be his first full year playing for the Seals. He was eighteen years old now. Even though he was still very thin, he was over six feet tall and weighed almost 190 pounds. He was still a boy, but he had the body of a man.

Seals manager Ike Caveney could tell that Joe was a good player, but he already had a shortstop and all the other positions were filled. Joe had to sit on the bench.

He didn't like it, but he didn't let his

frustration show. Joe was naturally quiet and private. The other players started calling him "Deadpan Joe" because he was so reserved.

A few games into the season, Joe got his chance. The Seals were in the field when the opposing batter hit a long drive to right field. Vince DiMaggio was the regular right fielder. At the crack of the bat, he could see the ball was over his head. He started to dash toward the fence.

In the 1930s, there were no warning tracks to tell outfielders they were a few feet from the wall. The walls weren't padded, either. Outfielders chasing long fly balls had to be extra careful about crashing into a wall.

Vince went back and made a spectacular one-handed diving catch. But when he came down, he landed heavily on his shoulder. He knew immediately that his throwing arm was hurt.

The Seals ran out to right field to help Vince back to the dugout. His day was finished. A doctor was summoned to examine him. It would be a few weeks before he would be able to throw a baseball again. Joe felt terrible for his brother.

Manager Ike Caveney paced the dugout trying to decide what to do next. He only had a few extra players, and he wanted to have them available in case he needed a pinch hitter. He looked up and down the Seals bench. "DiMaggio!" he barked. "Go play right field."

"But, Skip," Vince protested, "I'm hurt."

"Not *you!*" Caveney shouted. "Your kid brother."

Joe DiMaggio looked up suddenly. It took a moment or two for the manager's order to sink in. Joe was a shortstop. He had never played any other position. It hadn't occurred to him that he would ever take over if Vince got hurt.

"I–I don't know how to play the outfield," Joe stammered.

"You'd better learn fast," Vince said, handing Joe his glove.

*   *   *

Joe may not have known how to play the outfield, but he picked it up fast. Almost right away, he felt comfortable out in right field. He liked having a big, wide, open area he could roam around in, chasing down fly balls. He liked uncorking the long throw to third base or home plate to gun down a sliding base runner. Those throws were so much easier for Joe than the throw from shortstop to first base that he'd struggled with so much.

Within a few games, Joe had learned the ins and outs of his new position and turned himself into a fine outfielder.

Joe had always been a good hitter. His hitting got even *better* when he got the chance to play every day.

On May 28, 1933, Joe got a single. It wasn't any big deal, really. Just an ordinary grounder up the middle and into the outfield. Nobody thought anything about it at the time. Joe went one for four that day.

The next game he got another hit. Again, there was nothing special about it. The following game, Joe got two hits.

Getting hits in three straight games is pretty common. Baseball players do it all the time. But Joe kept hitting, getting hits in the fourth, fifth, sixth, and seventh games after that. He was feeling very good at the plate. He was seeing the ball well.

Seals fans started to notice that Joe was swinging a hot bat. When he had made at least one hit in fifteen straight games, people started mentioning that Joe was on a hitting streak.

One of the San Francisco newspapers did some research and discovered that the longest hitting streak in Pacific Coast League history was forty-nine games. It seemed unreachable.

A hitting streak is very hard to keep going. Even the best players have a bad day once in a while. Sometimes a fielder "robs" a hitter by making a great play. Other times the pitcher decides not to give a hot hitter anything good to hit and walks him.

Even a hitter swinging a very hot bat only hits about .400—which means he fails in six out of every ten at bats.

It seemed like it would only be a matter of time before Joe's hitting streak would come to an end.

But Joe kept hitting. Twenty games. Twenty-five games. Thirty games. Joe was so hot that even when he hit a ball poorly, it seemed to find a spot on the field where nobody could catch it.

When Joe's hitting streak reached thirty games, people who had never been to a game began flocking to Seals Stadium to see if Joe would get a hit. His picture appeared in the paper every day. Strangers recognized him when he walked down the streets of San Francisco. He was becoming a local celebrity.

As Joe began closing in on the record of forty-nine consecutive games with a hit, the pressure began to mount. All eyes were on him all the time. Fans began asking him how long the streak would last. People no longer seemed to care whether or not the Seals won the game. All that mattered was if Joe got his hit that day.

On July 13, Joe had reached the forty-eighth-game mark. One more game with a hit and he would tie the Pacific Coast League record. As the Seals warmed up for the game, everyone watched Joe's face to see if they could spot signs of tension. As usual, he was the same quiet, shy player as always.

When Joe came to the plate in the first inning, the crowd began to buzz. Fans were asking the people next to them if they thought Joe would crack under the pressure.

There were two outs. Joe looked at a couple of pitches without taking a swing, then hit a routine grounder to short. The crowd sat back, disappointed, and waited to see what would happen the next time Joe came to bat.

It happened in the fourth inning. This time there was a runner at second base. Joe wanted desperately to drive him in, but he got under the ball a little and hit an easy fly to left field. Once again, the crowd settled back into their seats.

Joe came up again in the seventh inning. A hush fell over the stands. Fans who understood the game realized that Joe might not get another chance to bat in this game. If he didn't get a hit right now, the streak could be over.

Joe pumped his bat back and forth smoothly as he waited for the first pitch. He reminded himself not to get overanxious. He didn't have to swing at the first pitch, even if it was a good one.

But it *was* a good one, and Joe *did* swing. He hit a wicked liner that jumped off the bat so fast, the fans didn't have the chance to stand up and see the ball—

112

Caught! The third baseman made a desperate dive, and the ball stuck in his glove.

A gasp came from the crowd. Joe's shoulders slumped slightly. He jogged back to the Seals' dugout as the crowd rose to give him a standing ovation. He had given it his best shot. He hit the ball hard. He just hit it in the wrong place. Some of the fans got up to leave.

The Seals weren't able to get a rally going in the eighth inning. When they came to bat in the ninth, many fans pulled out their scorecards. Joe was scheduled to bat seventh that inning. If the Seals went down one, two, three, Joe's hitting streak was over. But if they started a rally, Joe could get one more turn at bat. Four of the Seals ahead of him would have to reach base. It wasn't very likely.

The first hitter for the Seals struck out. Hearts sank all over the ballpark. It wasn't looking good.

But the next hitter walked, and the one after him singled. There was a pop-up for the second out, but then one of the Seals doubled home a run and the batter after him was hit by a pitched ball.

Incredibly Joe DiMaggio would get one more chance to keep his hitting streak alive. A few of the people who had left the ballpark rushed back after hearing what was happening on the radio. The crowd that remained moved to the edges of their seats.

The pitcher worked carefully to Joe. Ball one. Strike one. The pitcher didn't want to give him anything too good to hit, but he didn't want to walk him, either. He knew that if he walked Joe in this situation, the fans would never let him hear the end of it.

Ball two. Strike two. Ball three.

The count was full. One more ball and Joe would walk. One more strike and he would be a strikeout victim. The pressure was on. The crowd was silent. The pitcher checked the sign and went into his windup. Joe tightened his grip on his bat.

The pitch was a little low, but not low enough that Joe could watch it go by. He took a healthy cut at it, and once again he connected.

This time the ball didn't rocket toward the third baseman. It soared off toward left field. The left fielder started backing up, then saw it was going to be over his head. He leaped for it, but the ball hit the left-field fence on the fly and bounced back toward the field. Joe pulled into second base with a standup double.

The streak was still alive! Joe had hit into an incredible forty-nine games in a row. The crowd took a full fifteen minutes to stop cheering.

The next day, Joe broke the record and the crowd cheered even longer. This time he singled in the first inning, so everyone could breathe easily the rest of the game. Joe now owned the record: fifty consecutive games with a base hit.

The streak didn't stop there. Joe kept hitting. Fifty-two. Fifty-four. Fifty-six. It was amazing. Scouts from all the major-league teams started coming around to Seals Stadium to see if what they were hearing about this DiMaggio kid could be true. *Nobody* gets a hit every day.

Finally, on July 25, the streak came to an end. Joe went hitless in four at bats. But he had made at least one hit in sixty-one consecutive games. Nobody had ever done it before, and nobody has ever done it since—in any league.

For those few months in the summer of 1933, Joe DiMaggio had helped the people of San Francisco forget about the Depression for a little while. Italian Americans were particularly proud that one of their own had accomplished this amazing feat.

The mayor of San Francisco presented Joe with a watch at a special day in Joe's honor.

The entire DiMaggio family was there, even Giuseppe.

At the end of his first full season with the Seals, Joe had some impressive statistics next to his name. In addition to his hitting streak, he had hit .340, with 28 home runs, 13 triples, 45 doubles, and 169 runs batted in. In right field, he had thrown out 32 base runners, which led the Pacific Coast League.

It was clear that Joe DiMaggio could do all five things a baseball player has to do—hit, hit for power, run, throw, and field.

Major-league teams were drooling all over themselves for the chance to buy Joe's contract from the San Francisco Seals. Unless something terrible happened, the sportswriters gossiped, Joe could make it to the major leagues by 1935 and become the highest-paid rookie sensation in baseball history.

And then something terrible happened.

Damaged Goods

Joe's second season with the San Francisco Seals looked like it was going to be a repeat of his first one. He started 1934 on a hitting tear. Joe was batting over .340. By July, he had twelve home runs.

Opposing base runners learned not to try for extra bases on a hit to right field, because Joe would gun them down. Every major-league team had contacted the Seals about buying Joe's contract for 1935.

Because Joe was doing so well in right field, the Seals traded his brother Vince to

Hollywood, another team in the Pacific Coast League. Joe felt bad about that. He had signed with the Seals in the first place so he could play on the same team as Vince. If he hadn't played so well, Vince probably would not have been traded.

But Joe tried to get that thought out of his mind. Every player, he realized, had to play the best he could. Players get traded from one team to another all the time. Teammates just have to get used to it, even if they are brothers. Joe couldn't expect that he and Vince would play on the same team forever.

One sunny afternoon at the end of July, the Seals had a doubleheader. Joe played both games, and played well. He was tired after five hours of baseball. His older sister Nellie had invited him over for dinner at her home that night, and he was looking forward to a relaxing evening.

There was a bus that went from Seals

Stadium almost directly to Nellie's apartment. After he showered and changed his clothes in the locker room, Joe hopped on the bus and took a seat. To avoid being pestered by fans requesting autographs, he pulled a hat down over his eyes and buried his head in a newspaper.

The bus was crowded. People jammed onto the seats on either side of Joe, pinning him in tightly. After a few minutes, he noticed that his foot had fallen asleep. Joe kept tapping his toe to "wake it up."

Looking out the window of the bus, Joe saw that it was approaching his sister's stop. As the bus began to slow down, Joe got up quickly.

He wasn't sure if he heard the cracks first or felt the pain. There were four sharp cracks, like the sound of pistol shots. The cracks came from Joe's left knee. He collapsed to the floor of the bus, in excruciating pain.

"Help that young man!" a lady shouted as a crowd of people gathered around Joe.

"Hey, that's the DiMaggio kid!" another rider exclaimed. "He plays for the Seals!"

Joe was in agony. The driver stopped the bus, and several of the passengers carried Joe off. An ambulance was called, and Joe was taken to the hospital.

Doctors examined Joe's knee, but they didn't see the seriousness of the injury. Hot towels and salt packs were wrapped around Joe's knee. He was sent home, hobbling and moaning with pain.

The next morning, when Joe got out of bed, his knee collapsed under him again. Another doctor examined it and told Joe he had torn the ligaments of his left knee. A ligament is a band of tissue that connects bones together. Joe had to wear an aluminum splint that covered his whole leg.

"When will I be able to play ball again?" Joe asked the doctor. "How long until I can run?"

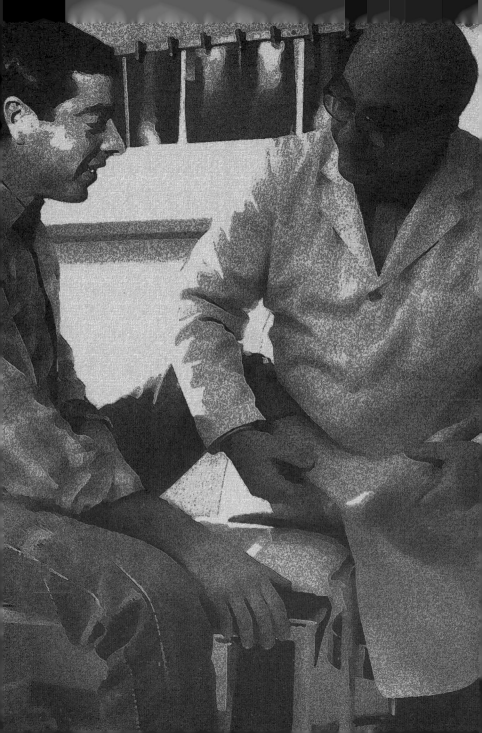

"Son," the doctor replied, "I don't know if you'll *ever* be able to run again."

The news about Joe DiMaggio's injury swept through baseball like a hurricane. The major-league teams that had been so interested in Joe suddenly stopped calling. Knee injuries were *serious,* much more serious than they are today. If a guy had a bum knee, it didn't matter if he was a good hitter or a good fielder. He couldn't run.

The word was out: Joe DiMaggio was "damaged goods."

His 1934 season finished, Joe sat on the Seals' bench and cheered his teammates on. When the cast was taken off his leg after three weeks, Joe couldn't bend his knee at all. His leg was very weak.

As he watched the next eighty-six games, Joe thought about his future. He was only nineteen years old. He didn't want to work for his father's fishing business. He didn't want to go back to school. He didn't like any of the jobs he had tried. There was only one thing he really liked to do, and that was play baseball.

But it looked like his career as a baseball player was over.

Taking a Chance

The mood in the offices of the New York Yankees was somber. The 1934 baseball season had ended, and the Yankees had finished second for the second year in a row.

Second place may have been pretty good for most teams, but not for the Yankees. From 1921 to 1932, they had come in first place seven times. Second place was not good enough.

Even worse, the great Babe Ruth, who had carried the team on his big shoulders all those years, was finished. Babe had become old, fat, and slow, and the Yankees didn't even offer him a contract for 1935.

A meeting was arranged in the offices at Yankee Stadium to discuss the future of the team. The Yankee owner, Colonel Jacob Ruppert, sat at the head of a long table. Surrounding him were manager Joe McCarthy and two Yankee scouts, Bill Essick and Joe Devine.

"Gentlemen," the Colonel addressed the group. "I don't like finishing second. Second place is for losers. The New York Yankees are not losers. So what are we going to do about it?"

"I need a new right fielder, for starters," said manager McCarthy. "Even though Ruth was washed up, we still got twenty-two homers out of him this year."

"We need more than just a right fielder," the Colonel said. "We need somebody who can get people excited enough to come out to the ballpark every day. Ruth sure put those fannies in the seats."

126

"We need the next Ruth," Bill Essick commented.

"There ain't no next Ruth," insisted Joe Devine. "He was one of a kind."

"What about a trade to bring another star to New York?" suggested the Colonel.

"The only guy we have that anybody wants is Lou Gehrig," replied McCarthy.

"Gehrig can't carry the team by himself," Devine noted.

"I'm not giving up Gehrig," Colonel Ruppert said.

"Lou's over thirty, you know," McCarthy said. "He's only got a few years left. Maybe we can trade him now and get two younger guys in return."

"We keep Gehrig," insisted Colonel Ruppert. "Who's the best young prospect out there?"

"Well, there's this kid DiMaggio on the San Francisco Seals," said Bill Essick. "But he busted his knee and missed most of the season.

Freak accident. Fell off a bus or something. It's a shame."

"How good was he before he busted his knee?" asked Ruppert.

"I saw the kid play," Joe Devine said with a smile. "He was sensational. He could do it all—run, throw, field, hit, hit with power. Slugs a ton of homers and never strikes out. His glove is like a magnet for baseballs."

"This is the kid who hit into sixty-one straight games," added Bill Essick. "He's got a couple of brothers who are pretty good ballplayers, too."

"Yeah, I remember the kid's name," the Colonel said. "We've got a lot of Italians in New York, too. They'll love him. Will his knee recover?"

"Hard to say," Joe Devine explained. "We had a doctor look at it in Boston. He wouldn't give us any guarantees, but he said DiMaggio is young enough that he might heal up like brand new."

"How old is this DiMaggio kid?" asked the Colonel.

"He turns twenty in November," replied Joe Devine, checking his notes.

"I say DiMaggio with a bad knee is better than nine out of ten guys with two good knees," Bill Essick said, making the others laugh.

"Is anybody else chasing him?" asked the Colonel.

"Everybody was," claimed Devine. "The Cubs and the Red Sox were all over him last year. But when he tore up his knee, they tore up their offers. Everybody got scared off."

"Maybe *we* should be scared off," McCarthy said.

"Maybe," agreed the Colonel. "Or maybe if everybody else is scared off, we can get this DiMaggio kid cheap. How much do the Seals want for him?"

"They were asking seventy-five thousand dollars," Joe Devine replied, again checking his notes. "But that was before he got hurt. Now I think we can get him for twenty-five thousand. And I'm pretty sure the kid wants to play for the Yankees. His lifelong dream, you know."

"Of *course* he wants to play for the Yankees," McCarthy said. "Who wouldn't want to play for the Yankees?"

Colonel Ruppert sat back in his chair and puffed on his cigar. He was a millionaire in a time when many men didn't have a dollar to their name. But he was very careful with his money. Finally he leaned forward to address the group. "Make that offer to the Seals," he ordered. "If DiMaggio's knee heals, we'll look like a bunch of geniuses. If he flops, at least we didn't risk much to get him."

Off to Spring Training

Taking the risk that Joe's knee would heal proved to be one of the smartest decisions the New York Yankees ever made. Joe recovered from his injury completely.

Playing for the Seals while his knee got better, Joe came within two points of hitting .400 in 1935. He slugged 34 home runs and drove in 154 runs. Bad knee or not, he stole 24 bases in 25 attempts. The San Francisco Seals won the Pacific Coast League pennant.

The baseball world—and the New York Yankees in particular—anxiously prepared to meet the next sensation.

"Here is the replacement for Babe Ruth," wrote sportswriter Dan Daniel in the *New York World-Telegram*.

It was a chilly day in February of 1936. The wind was whipping off San Francisco Bay. A crowd of people gathered outside the DiMaggio house. Word had spread around the neighborhood that one of the DiMaggio brothers was leaving home to go play baseball with the New York Yankees.

Inside, Joe nervously packed his bags. He was used to playing ball in front of crowds, but this was different. Everybody wanted to talk to him. They wanted to congratulate him, wish him luck, pinch his cheeks. Joe, still very shy, wished there was a back door he could sneak out.

By 1935, some of the DiMaggio children

had homes of their own. But all of them gathered at their parents' house on Taylor Street to see Joe off. Mrs. DiMaggio and Joe's sisters were obviously proud of Joe, fussing over him and making sure he had packed everything he'd need for the long trip to spring training in St. Petersburg, Florida.

His older brothers Michael and Thomas clapped Joe on the back. They wished him well, but there was a trace of sadness in their eyes. Both of them had been terrific athletes when they were younger. If they hadn't chosen to join their father in the family fishing business, that might be *them* heading off to the major leagues.

Vince and Dom had mixed feelings about Joe leaving, too. Ever since they were little, they had dreamed of playing in the majors. Now Joe was getting the chance. Vince and Dom wished it was *them* packing their suitcases.

At the same time, watching Joe gave them hope. If they kept trying, they

133

thought, maybe *their* turn would come.

Finally, after everyone else in the family had wished him luck, Joe's father came into his room. "I can't believe you've grown so big," Giuseppe DiMaggio told Joe, who now towered over his dad.

"Must be Mom's cooking."

"I guess maybe you weren't cut out to be a fisherman after all," Giuseppe said, sighing.

"I tried to like it, Papa," Joe said. "I really did. But you know how you always said the DiMaggios were fishermen and you felt that fishing was in your blood?"

"Yes."

"That's the way I feel about baseball, Papa. It's the only thing I was ever good at. It's the only thing I ever loved."

"I know, son."

Joe and his father were men of few words. An awkward silence fell between them until the elder DiMaggio finally broke it. "Can I give you a little advice, Giuseppe?" he asked.

"Sure, Papa."

"You gotta wait on the curveball better," Mr. DiMaggio said, getting into a batting stance. "Those big-league pitchers, they're gonna strike you out on that pitch."

"Papa!" Joe had to smile. "Where did you learn so much about baseball?"

"I've been studying," Mr. DiMaggio said. "I'm not so dumb. I know a few things." Then he hugged Joe very hard and encouraged him to do his best at spring training.

A car honked outside. Joe picked up his suitcase and walked out the front door with his father.

The crowd of people outside the DiMaggio house had surrounded the car in the middle of the street. It was a shiny new Ford sedan. Not many people could afford a car at all in 1936, much less a fancy one like this.

More importantly, there were two celebrities in the car: Yankee second baseman and shortstop Tony Lazzeri and Frank Crosetti.

Both veteran players were born and raised in San Francisco. They were also both Italian American like Joe. Lazzeri had offered to drive Crosetti and DiMaggio to spring training in his new car.

Kids were holding out pieces of paper for Lazzeri and Crosetti to sign. It wasn't every day that real, live, major-league baseball players stopped by the neighborhood. Fans were all over the car.

"Hop in, kid," Lazzeri shouted to Joe. "Or we'll never get out of here."

Joe climbed in the back seat and waved once more to his friends and family gathered in the street. The crowd in front of the car parted. Tony Lazzeri hit the gas, and the car roared away.

Joe had never been east of the Rocky Mountains before, but now he was going off on an adventure that would take him to Florida, New York City, and all around the country. He was twenty-one years old.

A Natural

Joe carefully peeled a twenty-dollar bill from his wallet and handed it to Frank Crosetti in the front seat of the car. The three Yankees had agreed to split the expenses of getting to spring training in Florida. Back in 1936, sixty dollars would cover food, gas, and lodging for a cross-country trip.

There were no big interstate highways in those days. Lazzeri had to drive on smaller roads. The trip to St. Petersburg would take about a week.

After driving about a hundred miles,

Lazzeri stopped the car and switched seats with Frank Crosetti. Crosetti drove a hundred miles, then pulled over to the side of the road. "Your turn, kid," Crosetti told Joe.

"My turn?"

"That's right."

"Uh, I forgot to tell you something," Joe said. "I can't drive."

"What?" Crosetti asked, turning around.

"I don't know how to drive," Joe repeated.

"What do you mean you don't know how to drive?" Lazzeri asked, annoyance in his voice. If Joe couldn't drive, he and Crosetti would have to drive more than a thousand miles each.

"I never learned."

"Kid, you're gonna drive," Crosetti said, pulling the car back onto the road. "You're gonna drive me crazy!"

A week later, the two exhausted veterans and the young rookie arrived in St.

138

Petersburg, Florida. Lazzeri drove straight to the Yankee spring training camp.

When they walked into the locker room, Joe was awestruck. Bill Dickey, Red Ruffing, and Lefty Gomez came over and introduced themselves. These were names that Joe had read in the newspaper. The great Lou Gehrig shook his hand and greeted him like an old friend. Joe couldn't believe it was really happening.

The equipment manager called Joe over and handed him a uniform. During the drive from San Francisco, Joe had been wondering what number he would be given. He knew that players who didn't have much chance of making the Yankees were usually given a high number, while top players received low numbers. Babe Ruth had worn number 3, for instance, and Lou Gehrig wore number 4.

Joe opened up the uniform that was handed to him. It was number 5.

Joe didn't have time to marvel about the

fact that he was a major-league player for the New York Yankees. Almost immediately reporters surrounded him and began pelting him with questions. Always shy, Joe didn't have much to tell them. Usually he supplied one-word answers to their questions.

"Say, Joe," one frustrated reporter asked, "how about giving me a quote?"

"A quote?"

Joe thought fast. Nobody had ever asked him for a quote before. He didn't even know what a quote *was*. It didn't have anything to do with baseball, he was sure of that.

Maybe the reporter meant "Coke" instead of "quote," Joe figured. He thought about giving the reporter a bottle of Coke, but stopped. What if he wasn't allowed to give out sodas to reporters? Why would a reporter be asking one of the players for a Coke, anyway?

"I don't think so," Joe said simply, and walked away.

* * *

Joe may not have had much to say to the press, but as usual his bat did the talking for him. In his first twenty at bats of spring training, he got twelve hits. When the regular season began, Joe ripped a single on the second pitch thrown to him. Later in that first major-league game, he got a triple and another single.

During the first few weeks of the season, Joe's bat was on fire. He got thirteen hits in first twenty-five at bats. He came to bat twice in one inning, and hit a home run each time. Most power hitters strike out a lot, but Joe hardly ever did.

Everybody had expected that Joe was going to hit well. What amazed the Yankee management and the press was the way Joe played the field.

Joe was a natural. He never seemed to make a mistake. He never dropped a fly ball or threw to the wrong base. Joe covered so much ground that he was moved from left

141

field to center field. He would play that position for the rest of his career.

It wasn't long before the whole baseball world was talking about the rookie sensation Joe DiMaggio. Yankee radio broadcaster Arch McDonald named him the Yankee Clipper because he patrolled the big center field at Yankee Stadium like the great ships that once sailed the Atlantic. Fans began to call him Joltin' Joe because of the way he socked the ball.

Naturally, Joe made the American League All-Star team. He also made the cover of *Time* magazine.

When his rookie season was over, Joe had produced 206 hits, 132 runs, and 29 homers in just 138 games, plus a .323 batting average. He threw out 22 base runners, more than any other outfielder in the league.

After finishing three games out of first place in 1935, the Yankees cruised to the pennant by nearly twenty games in 1936. Led by

Joe DiMaggio and Lou Gehrig, they won the World Series for the first time in four years.

"Instead of being the second Babe Ruth," wrote James M. Kahn in *The New York Times*, "here is a young man who is going to be the first Joe DiMaggio."

When Joe came back to San Francisco after his rookie season with the Yankees, he was surprised by the greeting he received. A brass band was there to meet him at the train station. Fans swarmed around asking for his autograph. There was a parade to city hall in his honor. The mayor of San Francisco gave a speech saying how proud his hometown was of a local boy who had made good. Mr. and Mrs. DiMaggio, of course, were more proud than anyone.

"Remember all those times I told you baseball was a waste of time, and how you should be out fishing with me?" Giuseppe asked Joe.

"Yeah."

"I was wrong," Giuseppe admitted. "You did good. I'm so proud of you."

"It was all because of you, Pop."

"Me?"

"Yeah," Joe told his dad. "I was waiting on that curveball, just like you told me to."

The two DiMaggios hugged again and held on to each other for the rest of the parade.

An Amazing Career

Every few years an exciting young rookie comes along and has a sensational season. Most of the time, he doesn't have another one. Either he becomes an ordinary player or he fizzles out of the big leagues entirely. That didn't happen with Joe DiMaggio.

In his second season, Joe raised his batting average to .346 and slammed a league-leading forty-six homers. Once again, he led the Yankees to a World Series victory.

They won the World Series again in 1938, and yet again in 1939, when Joe won the batting title and was named Most Valuable Player. That made it four championships in four seasons. Even the great Babe Ruth never had accomplished that.

In 1941, Joe had one of the most amazing summers in baseball history. It started on May 15 when he singled off Ed Smith of the Chicago White Sox. Joe's bat got hot as the hits kept flying off it. In game after game, he got at least one hit.

The New York Yankee record for consecutive games with a hit was twenty-nine, and Joe smashed it quickly. Then he passed Ty Cobb's American League record of forty straight games. The modern major-league record was forty-two by George Sisler, and Joe topped that, too.

Somebody discovered that back in 1897 Wee Willie Keeler had hit in forty-four straight games for the Baltimore Orioles.

The news didn't bother Joe. He passed Keeler, too.

Joe's hit streak attracted even more attention than the streak he had with the Seals in 1933. Back then, he was the talk of San Francisco. This time, Joe was the talk of the whole *nation*.

People sat by their radios every day through June to find out what Joe did that day. When somebody asked, "Did he get his hit yet?" everyone knew what they were talking about. The question on every American's mind was: How long can Joe keep the streak alive?

As the streak grew, a hit song was heard all over America . . .

> "He started baseball's famous streak that's got us all aglow.
> He's just a man and not a freak, Joltin' Joe DiMaggio."

The streak was turning Joe into a folk hero. When it reached fifty games, people began to suspect that he must be superhuman.

The thing that makes a hitting streak so difficult is that the hitter isn't allowed to have a bad day. When Mark McGwire hit an amazing seventy home runs in 1998, he went as many as nine games in a row without a homer. Joe had to get a hit in every single game.

Joe was up to fifty-six straight games with a hit when the Yankees came to Cleveland on July 17 to play a series against the Indians. Joe hit the ball hard, but third baseman Ken Keltner made two great plays to rob him of hits. The streak was finally over.

Joe DiMaggio wasn't finished, though. He got hits in his next seventeen straight games. If not for the game in Cleveland, the streak would have reached seventy-four games.

Most other "unbreakable" records have been broken. Babe Ruth's astonishing record of sixty homers in a season and 714 in a career were broken by Roger Maris and Hank Aaron respectively. Lou Gehrig's record of 2,130 consecutive games played was broken by Cal Ripken, Jr.

But more than half a century has passed since Joe DiMaggio had his fifty-six-game hit streak, and so far nobody has come within eleven games. This is a record that may live forever. Joe will always be remembered most of all because of "the streak."

While Joe was streaking and winning his second MVP Award, the Yankees won the World Series again.

Joe DiMaggio was twenty-eight years old now. That is the age when most athletes are in their prime. He could look forward to having his best seasons. But it didn't work out that way.

Two months after the 1941 season was over, Japan bombed the American naval base at

Pearl Harbor and the United States entered World War II. Like many ballplayers, Joe enlisted to fight for his country in 1942.

He didn't see any action, but while Joe was in the service, he missed the 1943, 1944, and 1945 seasons entirely.

Many of the players who came back after World War II were no longer effective. They had been injured or simply became too old. But Joe came back after the war and won his third MVP Award in 1947. He also tied the American League record for outfielders by making only one error in 141 games.

The Yankees, naturally, won the World Series once again.

While Joe was becoming a star with the Yankees, Vince and Dom DiMaggio didn't give up baseball. They kept playing and getting better. One of the most satisfying things for Joe DiMaggio was seeing his brothers reach the major leagues.

In 1937, Vince was signed by the Boston Braves, a team that once was part of the National League. Vince was not a big-league star. In fact, he led the league in strikeouts six times! But he did hit 125 home runs in a career that lasted ten years.

Dom DiMaggio did even better than Vince. He was signed by the Boston Red Sox in 1940 and played for them eleven seasons. Dom (nicknamed "the Little Professor" because he wore glasses) hit over .300 four times and scored over one hundred runs six times. He even outhit Joe in 1946 and 1950.

Dom was a great fielder, and became the first outfielder ever to make 500 putouts in a season. He also led the American League in stolen bases in 1950.

If not for his more famous brother, Dom would have been considered one of the best players in baseball. When the Yankees faced the Red Sox, the two DiMaggio brothers had a friendly rivalry. Twice they played alongside each other in baseball's annual All-Star game.

During Joe's thirteen seasons with the Yankees, the team won the American League pennant an incredible ten times. In nine of those ten years, the Yankees won the World Series.

Joe compiled a lifetime batting average of .325 with over 2,000 hits, over 1,500 runs batted in, and 361 home runs. If he hadn't missed three seasons during World War II, he undoubtedly would have been a member of the 500 home run club.

Injuries, which had started bothering him way back in his days with the San Francisco Seals, got worse and worse. During his career, Joe had a sore arm, a burned foot, infected tonsils, an abscessed tooth, ulcers, pneumonia, and painful bone spurs in his right heel.

In 1951, at the age of thirty-seven, Joe DiMaggio decided to retire as a player. He could have played a few more seasons, but Joe didn't want young fans to see him as a fading star. He wanted people to remember him at his best.

"When baseball is no longer fun," he told reporters after the final game of the 1951 World Series, "it's no longer a game, and so, I've played my last game."

In his last at bat of that game, Joe hit a double. Naturally, the Yankees won the World Series again. They would retire Joe's number 5 on opening day of the 1952 season. At that time, only Babe Ruth and Lou Gehrig had received such an honor.

Call it luck or call it good judgment, but for forty-five years, whenever it came time for the leader of the New York Yankees to leave the game, there was a new young star to replace him.

Babe Ruth ruled all of baseball through the 1920s. When Ruth faded from the scene in the 1930s, Lou Gehrig led the team to victory. When Gehrig tragically got the disease that bears his name, Joe DiMaggio came along to lead the team to the World Series through the 1940s.

When DiMaggio's career came to a close, the Yankees had another exciting youngster waiting to take his place in center field. His name was Mickey Mantle, and he continued the Yankee winning tradition through the 1950s and into the early 1960s.

In the forty-five years from 1920 to 1965, the New York Yankees won an amazing twenty-nine pennants.

After Baseball

As you know, Joe DiMaggio was a very reserved and private person. When his playing days were over, Joe dropped out of sight for a while. He lived quietly with his sister, Marie, in a house he had bought for his parents when he became a star with the Yankees.

But soon Joe was back in the headlines, and the headlines were bigger than ever.

In 1953, Joe met possibly the most famous woman in the world—actress Marilyn Monroe. Despite Joe's shyness and Marilyn's need for attention, the two got along well.

Soon they fell in love and were married in January of 1954.

It was not Joe's first marriage. He had been married in the early 1940s to actress Dorothy Arnold. Joe and Dorothy had had a child named Joe, Jr. The couple had divorced in 1944.

When Joe married Marilyn Monroe ten years later, it was a huge event. The public found the marriage of two of the most famous people in the world to be fascinating. Reporters followed them everywhere they went.

The marriage didn't last a year. Marilyn wanted Joe to support her soaring career as a movie star. Joe wanted Marilyn to stay home.

Even after they divorced, though, Joe and Marilyn remained good friends. When Marilyn Monroe passed away in 1962, Joe took care of her funeral and arranged for six red roses to be put on her grave "twice a week, forever." He never married again.

After his marriage with Marilyn Monroe was over, Joe DiMaggio didn't disappear. He was inducted to the National Baseball Hall of Fame in 1955. He was a coach and vice president for the Oakland A's for a short time. He was named the "greatest living ball player" in 1969.

He became famous to a new generation of fans who saw him on television as the commercial spokesman for the Bowery Savings Bank in New York and the Mr. Coffee coffeemaker.

In 1976, Joe was presented with the Medal of Freedom by President Gerald Ford.

As the years went by, Joe's personal appearances became more and more infrequent. He could be seen at Yankee Stadium, throwing out the ceremonial first pitch to open baseball season. But he stopped playing in old-timers' games in 1988. He didn't want people to remember him as an old man.

In 1992 he started the Joe DiMaggio Children's Hospital Foundation.

For years, Joe had smoked three packs of cigarettes a day. In the mid-1990s he developed lung cancer. He fought the disease for a long time, but in the end it defeated him.

Joe DiMaggio, at age eighty-four, died a month before Opening Day of the 1999 baseball season, just after midnight on March 8. He was buried in the city he always loved, San Francisco.

An American Hero

When it comes to baseball statistics, people usually talk about how many home runs a player hit or how high his batting average was. But Joe DiMaggio had one very little known statistic that is astonishing.

In his major-league career, Joe hit 361 home runs while striking out only 369 times. His home run total and his strikeout total are almost identical.

Sluggers usually strike out a lot because they have to swing the bat very hard to hit the ball a long way. Babe Ruth struck out 1,330 times in his career. Mickey Mantle struck out 1,710 times. Reggie Jackson struck out an incredible 2,597 times. For a power hitter to strike out only 369 times in his whole career is *amazing*.

If you look in the record books, you will see other players who hit more home runs than Joe DiMaggio. Lesser known players have had a higher lifetime batting average, more hits, and played more seasons.

So why is Joe DiMaggio one of the most famous players in the history of the game, one of the most famous Americans of the twentieth century? Why does every kid at school know his name even though he played decades before they were born?

Because statistics don't tell the whole story. Joe DiMaggio, by the way he played and the way he behaved, represented what we think of as American values: honesty, dignity, graciousness, and fair play.

In most of the things we do, there is

usually a right way and a wrong way to do it. Joe DiMaggio, whether he was trying to or not, always seemed to do the right thing.

In his book *The Old Man and the Sea*, Ernest Hemingway wrote, "I must have confidence and I must be worthy of the great DiMaggio who does all things perfectly . . . "

On the field, Joe always gave his best no matter what the score was. A reporter once asked him why he kept playing so hard even though the Yankees had already won the pennant. DiMaggio replied, "There may be some kids out there who may be seeing me play for the first time. I owe them my best."

When he lost, he didn't whine or complain or throw a tantrum. He never argued with umpires, fans, or reporters. He never lost his dignity.

When he was hurt, he played, anyway. And when the time had come that his skills were fading, he had the sense to get off the field before he embarrassed himself.

As good as he was, Joe never boasted of his accomplishments. He didn't chase publicity or try to get his name in the papers. He didn't pump his fist or do a silly dance after he hit a homer. He wasn't a show-off and he didn't mouth off. He was quiet. The less he said, the more people wanted to know about him. But he never even wrote an autobiography.

No matter how many times he was asked, he kept his private life private. He was never involved in a scandal. He respected the woman he loved, and didn't gossip about her after she passed away. He treated his parents well, even though they were not always entirely supportive of his career.

Joe DiMaggio looked cool, and he dressed cool, always in a suit and tie. He was voted one of the "best-dressed men" in America.

He was a hero to all Americans, but as a poor fisherman's son who made something of himself, Joe was especially admired by Italian Americans. Black people had Jackie

164

Robinson as their role model. Hispanics could look up to Roberto Clemente. Italian Americans had Joe DiMaggio.

It may be hard for young people today to imagine there was a time when people of Italian descent were discriminated against. Joe DiMaggio knew he was more than just a ballplayer. He represented Italians everywhere, and he made sure to show them in the best possible light.

These are all qualities that made Joe DiMaggio a genuine American hero. In the eyes of many people, he was the *last* real hero we've had.

In the late 1960s, singer Paul Simon wrote a song called "Mrs. Robinson" for the movie *The Graduate,* in which he mentions Joe DiMaggio.

Joe didn't like the song when he first heard it. He didn't understand it and thought that Simon might have been making fun of him. But he wasn't. He was trying to say that we need more people like Joe DiMaggio.

The day after Joe DiMaggio died, Paul Simon explained very simply what he had meant by the words in that song. He said, "We need heroes."

All of us look for role models to pattern our life after. In a perfect world those role models would be teachers, scientists, police officers, and others who make the world a better place every day. In the real world, our heroes tend to be famous people—movie stars, musicians, and athletes.

As long as we live in the real world, you couldn't pick a better hero than Joe DiMaggio.

A Joe DiMaggio Chronology

1914: Joe DiMaggio is born in Martinez, California, on November 25. He is the eighth of nine children.

1920: Joe attends Hancock Grammar School.

1927: Joe attends Francisco Junior High School.

1929: Joe attends Galileo High School. He leaves school after one year.

1932: Joe plays his first game for the San

Francisco Seals of the Pacific Coast
League.

1933: Joe gets a hit in sixty-one straight
games for the Seals.

1934: The New York Yankees purchase Joe
from the Seals for $25,000 and five
players.

1936: Joe gets three hits in his first major-
league game and goes on to hit .323.
The Yankees win the pennant and the
World Series.

1937: Joe's brother Vincent joins the Boston
Braves. Joe buys a restaurant on
Fisherman's Wharf in San Francisco
and calls it Joe DiMaggio's. Joe leads
the league in home runs and slugging
average. The Yankees win the pennant
and the World Series.

1938: Joe hits .324. The Yankees win the
pennant and the World Series.

1939: Joe wins the American League's Most
Valuable Player Award and batting

title, hitting .381. The Yankees win the pennant and the World Series. Joe marries actress Dorothy Arnold and buys his parents a new house.

1940: Joe hits .352 to win his second batting title. His brother Dom joins the Boston Red Sox.

1941: Joe sets the major-league record by hitting into fifty-six straight games. The record has never been approached. Joe hits .357, leads the league in RBIs, wins his second MVP, and the Yankees win the pennant and the World Series. Joe's only child, Joe DiMaggio, Jr., is born.

1942: Joe has an "off" year, hitting only .305. The Yankees win the pennant but lose the World Series.

1943: Joe enlists in the armed forces, which causes him to miss the next three seasons. Even without him, the Yankees still win the pennant and the World Series.

1944: Joe and Dorothy divorce.

1947: Joe wins his third MVP. The Yankees win the pennant and the World Series.

1948: Joe leads the league in home runs, home run percentage, and RBIs.

1949: Joe hits .346 and becomes the first player to earn one hundred thousand dollars for a season. The Yankees win the pennant and the World Series.

1950: Joe leads the league in slugging average. The Yankees win the pennant and the World Series.

1951: Joe retires from baseball after the season. The Yankees win the pennant and the World Series.

1953: Joe's brother Michael drowns in a fishing accident.

1954: Joe marries actress Marilyn Monroe in January. They divorce nine months later.

1955: Joe is elected to the National Baseball Hall of Fame.

1962: Marilyn Monroe dies.

1969: Joe is voted the "greatest living ballplayer."

1976: Joe is presented with the Medal of Freedom by President Gerald Ford.

1986: Vince DiMaggio dies. The restaurant Joe DiMaggio's closes.

1992: Joe starts the Joe DiMaggio Children's Hospital Foundation.

1998: Joe is honored with a special day at Yankee Stadium.

1999: Joe DiMaggio, at age eighty-four, dies on March 8 at his home in Hollywood, Florida.

Joe DiMaggio

Year	Team	Games	At Bats	Runs	Hits	Doubles
1936	Yankees	138	637	132	206	44
1937	Yankees	151	621	151	215	35
1938	Yankees	145	599	129	194	32
1939	Yankees	120	462	108	176	32
1940	Yankees	132	508	93	179	28
1941	Yankees	139	541	122	193	43
1942	Yankees	154	610	123	186	29
1946	Yankees	132	503	81	146	20
1947	Yankees	141	534	97	168	31
1948	Yankees	153	594	110	190	26
1949	Yankees	76	272	58	94	14
1950	Yankees	139	525	114	158	33
1951	Yankees	116	415	72	109	22
Total		1,868	7,324	1,471	2,360	409
World Series (10 years)		51	199	54	6	0
All-Star Games (11 years)		11	40	7	9	1

Career Statistics

Triples	Home Runs	Runs Batted In	Steals	Average
15	29	125	4	.323
15	46	167	3	.346
13	32	140	6	.324
6	30	126	3	.381
9	31	133	1	.352
11	30	125	4	.357
13	21	114	4	.305
8	25	95	1	.290
10	20	97	3	.315
11	39	155	1	.320
6	14	67	0	.346
10	32	122	0	.301
4	12	71	0	.263
139	386	1,632	31	.307
0	8	30	0	.249
0	1	6	1	.225